Mary Jane

By DOROTHY STERLING

Illustrated by ERNEST CRICHLOW

SCHOLASTIC BOOK SERVICES

Published by Scholastic Book Services, a division
of Scholastic Magazines, Inc., New York, N. Y.

Copyright © 1959 by Dorothy Sterling. This edition is published by Scholastic Book Services, a division of Scholastic Magazines, Inc., by arrangement with Doubleday & Company, Inc.

8th printing............December 1968

Printed in the U.S.A.

CONTENTS

For Phil
whose understanding helped
me write this book.
D. S.

On the farm

1

It was Mary Jane's last week on the farm. Purple asters were blooming in the fields. Katy-dids were singing their end-of-summer song. And Mamma had written that she was coming on Thursday to carry Mary Jane back home.

When Mary Jane was a little girl, too little to know about East and West and the earth turning on its axis, she thought that the sun rose on the road in front of Grampa's farm and set in the pine forests that covered the mountain slopes in the distance. In High Ridge where she lived most of the year, the sun never seemed to rise and set. It was just there, above the buildings on nice days and then, when it was time to go in for supper, it disappeared. Only you never saw it go. On the farm you could follow its course all day long.

When Mary Jane was a little girl, the whole

family spent summers on Grampa's farm. Now
Lou Ellen was a nurse in a hospital in the
North, coming home only at Christmas time,
and James was off studying to be a lawyer like
Daddy. Now Mary Jane was big, big enough to
know about the earth's rotation and to spend
the summer on the farm alone with Grampa.

Grampa's farm was different from other
farms. All the farmers nearby planted tobacco,
but Grampa planted only what he liked — vegetables for the kitchen, corn for the chickens,
and flowers to pleasure his eyes.

If the rabbits nibbled his cabbages, he just
shrugged his shoulders. "They're entitled to a
share for looking so pert when they zigzag
across the grass," he said.

If the blue jays and redbirds and crows
swooped down to eat his chicken feed, he put
out more corn and sang a song that he'd learned
when he was a boy. The two of them, Mary
Jane and Grampa, would watch the birds eating
and sing, off-key, but good and loud:

"Hi, says the red bird sitting on a fence.
 Once I courted a handsome wench.
 She proved fickle and from me fled
 And ever since then my head's been red.

"Hi, says the chicken hawk to the crow.
If you aren't black, well I don't know;
And ever since old Adam was born,
You've been known for stealing corn.

"Hi, says the blackbird to the crow.
What makes the white folks hate us so?
Ever since old Adam was born
It's been our trade to pull up corn.

"Hi, says the crow to the chicken hawk.
I understand your big loud talk;
You'd like to dive and catch a hen,
And I hope the farmer will shoot you then."

Grampa wouldn't even shoot chicken hawks. "Little bit of trouble they might cause with the chickens, that's nothing to the good they do feasting all year on grasshoppers and those mice your ma's so down on," he explained.

Mary Jane's mother, who'd been brought up in the city, shivered when she heard Grampa even talk about mice. "Better to be down on them than make pets of them, Pa Douglas," she retorted. "People say you open up your door in winter and tell all the field mice, 'Come in and keep warm.' Why, they say you even feed the weeds in your garden."

Grampa chuckled his slow deep chuckle. He didn't mind Mamma's teasing. Besides, what she said about the weeds was true. Alongside proper garden flowers, roses and hollyhocks that everyone grew, he planted rows of dandelions and sky-blue chicory and frilly white Queen Anne's lace.

Planting weeds wasn't as crazy as it sounded. A long time ago when Grampa was teaching at the state agricultural college he found ways to make rubber from dandelions and oil from seeds of other wild plants. Even now, although he had retired from the college and didn't teach any more, he still liked experimenting with plants, seeing if he could make them bigger or bluer or good to eat.

All summer long while Grampa fussed with his flower garden Mary Jane fussed with his animals. Mornings, she led Sophie the cow from the barn to the pasture and evenings she brought her safely back home again. She'd have milked her, too, except that her fingers weren't strong enough yet. But she could feed the chickens and the pigs and the awkward, long-legged calf that Sophie had borne in the spring, and she could take care of Curly.

At the beginning of the summer Curly had

been the runt of the pig litter, in danger of
being crushed to death by a careless mother
and starved by greedy brothers and sisters.
Mary Jane had taken him from the pen and fed
him milk from a baby's bottle and vegetables
from his very own dish. Now Curly was sleek
and fat and spoiled and he followed Mary Jane
all over the farm.

After supper, when Mary Jane and Grampa
sat on the back stoop watching the distant
mountains turn from green to blue to black,
Curly came too. He put his front feet on the
steps, grunting and straining until he'd climbed
up after them. Instead of admiring the sunset,
he poked his snout into Mary Jane's overalls
pocket to hunt for more things to eat. Mary
Jane scratched his head, right between the ears,
while Grampa sang "Mary had a little pig." His
voice rumbled along:

> "He followed her to school one day
> Which was against the rule.
> It made the children laugh and play
> To see a pig at school."

Mary Jane began to giggle. She laughed until

Curly squealed and Grampa tapped his pipe on the porch rail.

"My singing's not all that funny," he protested. "Even *your* singing's not that funny."

"It's not the singing." Mary Jane giggled again. "It's just — well — I got to thinking about Wilson High. It has millions of steps in front, marble, I guess — "

"Limestone," Grampa corrected her.

"Millions of limestone steps, and there's me walking up them with Curly following. . . ." This time Mary Jane laughed until there were tears in the corners of her eyes.

Grampa sucked on his pipe, waiting until she was quiet. "Been meaning to ask you about Wilson. How come you decided to go there 'stead of to Douglass, where Lou Ellen and James did their studying?"

Mary Jane was surprised at the question. Grampa knew perfectly well that Woodrow Wilson High was the best high school in High Ridge, if not in the whole state. "Last spring, before we graduated from Dunbar, the superintendent of schools talked at our assembly. He said the high school would be integrated in September. Those children who were graduating, we could go to Wilson if we wanted. Mamma and Daddy weren't so sure, but I knew right that day I was going to Wilson. And I am."

"Mmm." Grampa nodded. "Haven't said why."

"Because it's better than Douglass, that's why. Douglass has French, but Wilson has French and Latin. Douglass has just plain science — stuff I mostly know already. Wilson has physics and chemistry and biology. How'm I going to be a biologist if I don't go to Wilson?"

Grampa took the pipe out of his mouth and studied its bowl. "Some people," he observed, "seem to think I'm a biologist and I never went to Wilson."

"Oh, Grampa." Mary Jane was impatient now. "Things have changed since you were a boy. I know about how you had to study with your speller tied to the handles of a plow. And about washing dishes and scrubbing floors and cooking for people to earn money to go to school. But that's not the modern way. Now everybody can go, only some schools are better. I feel like I've got a right to go to Wilson.

"Any friends going along there with you?" Grampa asked.

"There are three, four older kids transferring

from Douglass to the high school, but the only ones going to junior high are Fred Jackson and me. I've known Fred all my life, but I wouldn't exactly call him a friend, him being a boy."

"I see." Grampa nodded once more.

Mary Jane wondered if he did see. He was asking practically the same questions Mamma and Daddy asked. "Likely you'll be lonesome," Mamma had said. "Only you and Fred in that great big school."

"Grownups!" Mary Jane burst out as if she were back home, arguing with Mamma. "Grownups think we just go to school to socialize. If I wanted to socialize I wouldn't have to go to school at all. I'm going to Wilson to get an education."

Said out loud like that, the words sounded big and brave. While she waited for Grampa to answer them, the sun dipped behind the mountains, leaving only a faint red glow on the distant peaks. Suddenly it was cold and dark on the stoop and Mary Jane shivered.

"Real feeling of fall in the air tonight," Grampa commented as he stood up, stretching. "You run put Curly to bed now and I'll get a fire started inside."

Curly had no intention of going to bed. He

trotted alongside Mary Jane until they reached the barn. Then he refused to budge. She had to get behind him and push hard to put him in the pen. After she locked the gate he squealed so pitifully that she stayed to scratch his head and comfort him.

Walking back to the house, she shook her head. Curly sure was spoiled. What was he going to do when she went home?

The story of Red Anne

2

BY THE TIME Mary Jane reached the kitchen there was a fire blazing in the fireplace and Grampa was sitting in his rocker with a basket of corn by his side. Flopping down on the hearth, Mary Jane stretched her hand for an ear of corn.

Listening to the hissing of the damp wood in the fireplace and the ticking of the mantelpiece clock, they shelled corn. Somewhere a cricket chirped and Mary Jane felt warm and comfortable, and not a bit like talking about Wilson High.

When Grampa edged forward in his chair as if he were about to say something, she headed him off. "Tell me a story. About Red Anne."

"Just thinking of her," Grampa admitted. "Only you know that story well as you know your name."

"Tell it," Mary Jane urged. "Red Anne was a little slave girl — "

"Red Anne was a little slave girl," Grampa repeated. "She was just a tiny thing when her mistress took her from her mamma and put her to work in the Big House. To mind the baby and sweep the floor and polish the silver — "

"And peel the potatoes. Only you forgot to say why she was called Red Anne," she reminded him.

"She was called Red Anne because she had a lovely red-brown skin. Because her daddy was an Indian."

Mary Jane squinted up at Grampa, trying to picture Red Anne. She must have had the same apricot-colored skin as he had, only black hair, black braids, where his was sparse and white. And no wrinkles, of course. "A Cherokee Indian," she added. "An Indian chief."

"I guess in stories every Indian's a chief." Grampa laughed. "Anyway, when Red Anne was about your age she got awful tired of working all the time and never seeing her mamma or having fun. She decided to run away. Only where could she go? She'd heard talk of a faraway place called North where slaves were free, but she didn't know the first thing about how

to get there. And she did know that there were
men patrolling the roads day and night, just
watching out for little slave girls who might
take it into their heads to run away."

"Then one day when she was dusting the
books in the parlor she decided to learn to read
and write," Mary Jane prompted.

Grampa nodded. "Seemed like white people,
they knew everything and that's why they
could boss the slaves. She figured that stealing
an education she maybe could boss herself.
Every afternoon when the young Master was
copying his homework she teased him into
teaching her. Of course he didn't realize what he
was doing, she being older than he was and a lot
smarter from having to work when she was so
little. She'd say, 'Bet you don't know what that
word is,' and he'd say 'house' or 'dog' or whatever it might be, showing off like boys do. Then
nights, when everybody was in bed, she prac-
ticed the writing in his books. Took time, but
finally she was able to read. She wasn't satisfied
with just the words in the speller. She learned
to read everything — books and newspapers and
letters that came to the Big House."

"Then she got too smart," Mary Jane suggested.

"Got to boasting to the people in the quarters until one of them told the Mistress. The Mistress was awful mad. Worst thing a slave could do was learn to read. Strictly against the law. Red Anne denied it, up and down and all around the clock, but the Mistress didn't know whether she was telling the truth. She took to leaving little notes around, sort of to trap Red Anne."

"Like 'There are cookies in the pantry' when Red Anne was awful hungry and never got to eat sweet things. And stuff about her mother and the other slaves. Only Red Anne didn't let on that she'd read them." No matter how often she heard the story, Mary Jane always got excited when Grampa got to this part.

"Until one day she read a letter from a man coming to see the Mistress about her. He planned to buy her and take her to Charleston with him. She went about her business that day, eyes blank, face smooth as butter. But all the time plans were circulating around in her head.

"After everyone was asleep, she took a piece of paper from the Mistress' desk and wrote herself a pass to show to the patrollers on the road. Signed the Mistress' name real carefully. Then, with nothing but some biscuits and a page from the boy's geography book, she ran away, clear up to New York City. And never did come back here to the South till after the Civil War."

Mary Jane waited while Grampa paused to fill his pipe. "You forgot the ending. You forgot to say, 'Red Anne was my mother.' When I was little and you said that, I got all over goose-pimples." She laughed.

"Red Anne was my mother — and your great-grandma," Grampa reminded her. "Seems as if education's always been important in our family."

There he went again, Mary Jane thought, edging back to talk about school. She tried to change the subject. "She was awful brave. I mean, setting out like that with nothing but a couple pieces of paper and the whole world against her."

Grampa blew a smoke ring that got bigger and bigger and bigger until it burst when it hit the ceiling. "People do what they have to do. Might be you're going to have to show a kind of bravery, too, one of these days."

Mary Jane frowned and half closed her eyes. She looked up at Grampa through her long lashes, but she didn't answer. Better let him talk and get it over with, she decided.

"Fact is, child, they'll be people at Woodrow

Wilson High School who aren't going to like
that pretty, cinnamon-colored skin of yours.
Might be they could be mean to you."

"Hi, says the blackbird to the crow,
What makes the white folks hate us so?"

Mary Jane sang, trying to make a joke out of
Grampa's talk.

Only Grampa didn't think it was funny. He
was being serious tonight. "Hate's part of it," he
pointed out, "and not knowing's another part.
They've got this picture of a Negro in their
minds and they just don't know you."

"Then they'll learn." Mary Jane shrugged her
shoulders as if she didn't care. "I'll be like some
ambassador from a foreign country."

"Sometime it's lonesome, being a foreign ambassador," Grampa cautioned. "The children in
school, they'll learn — and so will you. Likely it'll
hurt, some of that learning."

"Oh, Grampa." Mary Jane sat up straight,
her braids bobbing, her voice a little bit angry.
"Times have changed since Red Anne. There're
white girls on the next block I used to play with
when I was little. They say 'Hi' to me and I say
'Hi' to them. I'm not worried about school." She

tapped the hearth with a corncob. "I'm not worried," she repeated.

"Times have changed" — Grampa nodded — "and it's right for you to go to Wilson. But just come back to Red Anne for a minute. It's not true that she had the whole world against her. There were folks who helped her reach New York and helped her afterwards — farm ladies, preachers, ordinary folks. Of course she had to look sharp for them, and they weren't easy to find."

Mary Jane wriggled over to lean against Grampa's rocker, wondering what he was going to say next. "Sometimes you may get to feeling that the whole world's against *you*," he continued. "It's a terrible feeling. I've had it and I know. Can choke you, suffocate you, if you let it. And it won't be true, any more than it was true for Red Anne. That's what I want you to remember."

Rising abruptly, he began to poke around in the refrigerator, looking for the ice cream left from supper. "End of speech." He smiled.

Mary Jane let out her breath in a sigh. "I won't let it choke me," she promised. Then she jumped up to get plates and spoons from the cupboard.

The surprise

3

MARY JANE and Grampa never said another word about Wilson High. Not even when it was Last Night on the farm and she was bustling about packing her clothes and he was checking on her neck and ears and fingernails to make sure she was properly clean before Mamma came.

What with all the washing and the packing and the washing again, they had only a short time in front of the fire together. A short time to remember everything that had happened during the summer and to give instructions about Curly and make jokes.

Grampa sang:

> "Oh to be a cricket
> In a dusty thistle thicket."

And Mary Jane sang:

> "The sow got the measles
> And she died in the spring."

And they both laughed because neither of them could carry a tune and neither of them cared.

"No more lazying yourself under the hickory tree," Grampa teased.

"No more cleaning out the chicken coop. You'll have to do some work now," Mary Jane answered back. Cleaning the chicken coop was the one farm job she didn't like.

No more Grampa — no more Curly — no more Sophie — until next summer. But Mary Jane didn't feel sad when Mamma arrived in the morning as they were putting away the breakfast dishes. Mamma looked so trim and young and pretty in a new cotton dress that Mary Jane was glad she'd packed away her overalls. It would be good to wear dresses for a change and look in store windows on Main Street and do all the city things that city children did. The farm was nice, but so was home.

While Grampa stuffed the back of the car with tomatoes and eggs and flowers and greens and Mamma opened the closets to see if she had forgotten anything, Mary Jane skipped out to the barnyard. Curly's corkscrew tail waggled like a dog's when she kissed him good-by — after first making sure that Mamma wasn't looking. Mamma was understanding about most things, but she just didn't approve of kissing pigs — or letting them kiss you back. Wiping off the wet spot that Curly's snout had left on her cheek, Mary Jane ran to the car.

Grampa said, "Write me, child, when you take a notion," and kissed her in the exact same place Curly had. She hugged him, sniffing at the flower in the buttonhole of his faded blue shirt, and she waved good-by out of the car window until Mamma took the turn at the crossroads. When she couldn't see Grampa any more, she settled back in her seat to think about High Ridge.

Mamma was full of scraps of news. Lou Ellen wrote from the hospital that she was working on an interesting case. James hoped to get home for a weekend soon. Daddy had been busy with —

"Well, you'll see. It's a surprise for you."

No matter how hard Mary Jane begged, Mamma wouldn't tell the surprise. "You'll like it," she teased, "although these next couple days you won't have much chance to make use of it."

What in the world could "it" be? Mary Jane
was trying so hard to guess that she scarcely
paid attention as her mother told about all
the things they would have to do at home in
the next few days.

"Doctor . . . dentist . . . hairdresser . . ."

"Hairdresser? Whatever for?" Mary Jane sat
up when Mamma said that. Her hair touched
her shoulder blades when she unbraided it, and
it was one of her ambitions to let it grow until it
reached her waist. Like a princess in a storybook. Like Rapunzel, who let down her hair so
the king's son could climb up to the castle
where she was imprisoned.

"You're getting too big for pigtails," Mamma
explained. "I've been studying the way the girls
fix their hair now. Mostly they wear it short
or in a pony tail. I thought cut it a little in front
too, sort of fluffed up on your forehead and — "

"But, Mamma," Mary Jane protested. She
reminded her mother that Gwen and Peggy and
Laura and all her very best friends had braids.
"And mine are the longest of anybody's."

She didn't tell her mother about the princess
in the storybook, because Mamma would have
thought that was silly, but she argued for a

long time. And Mamma argued back, pointing out how much easier it would be to brush her hair in the morning if it were shorter.

"You're going to high school now," she said, "and the girls there set great store by how you look."

For a moment Mary Jane thought of asking if braids were all right for Douglass but not for Wilson High. Only that might start talk that she didn't want to hear. Besides, Mamma did know a lot more about fashions than she did and — well, not having braids would save time in the mornings, and well . . . Before they reached High Ridge she had agreed to the trip to the beauty parlor and was once more guessing about her surprise.

Everything at home looked small and trim and citified after the farm. Instead of scarlet trumpet vines climbing over weather-beaten shingles, there were gray stucco and shutters with fresh green paint and aluminum screen doors. Instead of barns and fields and chicken coop, there were rows of houses with tiny plots of grass in front and garages in back, each exactly alike for as far as you could see. Instead of oaks and hickories with spreading branches, there were spindly sidewalk trees with wrought-iron fences around them and privet hedges and scraggly hollies bunched against the porches.

But Mary Jane liked it. At home there were Mamma and Daddy and girls to play with, and stores and television. And upstairs in her bedroom there was the surprise.

The big old maple beds that she and Lou Ellen had always slept in were gone. In their place were day beds with broad bolsters to make them comfortable for sitting on. There were new bureaus built into the wall, and a desk with rows of drawers on either side and bookshelves above. And a real, honest-to-goodness dressing table with a mirror so that she wouldn't have to use the mirror in the bathroom when she fixed her hair. And a gooseneck lamp that could be used for studying at the desk or reading in bed.

Daddy had put up wallpaper with tiny bunches of flowers all over it, and Mamma had made a skirt for the dressing table and new curtains and pretty dark blue drapes that you closed by pulling a cord, like a stage curtain.

Mary Jane wanted to telephone Gwen and Peggy and Laura to come right over to see everything, but Mamma said no, there wasn't time.

"I want you to unpack while I fix supper. Daddy'll be home before you know it, and I'll have to hump some to get ready before he comes."

Mary Jane unpacked slowly. The bureau drawers smelled new and piny and she folded her clothes carefully as she put them away. Now that she was big and going to high school and had such a nice room she was going to be neat. No more kicking socks under the bed and leaving shoes in the middle of the floor and stuffing half-dirty sweaters in the drawers. Everything was going to be in its place the way Mamma wanted it to be.

By the time she was finished unpacking and had set the table, her regular job when she was home, she heard Daddy's key in the door. Then she forgot she was big and going to high school as she made a flying leap into his arms. Pretending that she was too heavy to hold, he dropped her on the couch.

"Let's get a good look at you," he said. "Your legs get longer by the minute."

"It's your forehead's getting longer," she teased. Truth to tell, Daddy was more than a little bit bald and didn't always like to be reminded of it. But tonight she could say anything without making him mad, because it was her first night home.

Supper was a First-Night-Home supper with steak and french fries and a three-layer cake with her favorite chocolate frosting.

"And no dandelion greens or wild chicory in the salad," Mamma pointed out. She didn't always approve of Grampa's cooking, especially when he experimented with wild plants. Mamma preferred proper food that came from the supermarket.

Mary Jane chattered away, telling about Sophie and the chickens and even about Curly. Although not "He followed her to school one day" and what Grampa said afterward. They filled her in on High Ridge news until long past time to clear the table.

Because it was First Night Home, Mamma excused her from helping with the dishes, and Mary Jane went into the living room to watch television. After two months away there were lots of programs to catch up on. It seemed like no time at all before Daddy said, "Time for bed, sugar," and she walked upstairs to sleep in her brand-new bed.

They say . . .

4

IN THE MORNING she had no chance to phone Gwen or Peggy or anybody. "Do you know all that we have to do today?" Mamma asked.

Mary Jane didn't know but she soon found out. Mamma bustled in and out of the department stores on Main Street, moving so quickly that Mary Jane had trouble keeping up with her. First a jacket, even though the old one that she'd gotten last spring was perfectly good, not too short in the sleeves or anything. Before she could stop to admire the new gray blazer, Mamma was in another department, studying racks and racks of skirts.

Mamma knew exactly what she wanted when it came to buying clothes. Sometimes the things that Mamma wanted weren't the ones that Mary Jane liked best. Mamma wouldn't even look at a felt skirt with little dog cutouts sewn all around. Instead, she picked out a charcoal gray without anything on it at all and a straight skirt in navy blue and sent Mary Jane into the dressing room to try them on. The straight skirt made her look grownup-tall, and when Mamma promised to buy a petticoat with a real hoop to wear under the gray one, Mary Jane gave up teasing for the skirt with the dogs.

Then Mamma picked out a white blouse and a blue shirt with a button-down collar and cuffs that needed cuff links, just as if there weren't drawers full of blouses at home. Of course Mary Jane didn't remind her of this, because if Mamma felt like buying new clothes she certainly felt like wearing them.

Next to the blouse counter were the sweaters. This time Mary Jane saw exactly what *she* wanted — a red sweater of soft, soft wool. Tugging at Mamma's elbow, she begged her to buy it.

"No red." Mamma was positive.

"Please, Mamma, please. It'll be fabulous with the gray skirt."

"It's too flashy for school," said Mamma, "it's just what they would expect you to wear."

Mamma consulted her list, again. "Socks. They're wearing knee socks this year, those heavy ribbed ones."

Mary Jane wondered if the "they" who were wearing knee socks and straight skirts and shoulder-strap bags and dickies this year were the same "they" who expected her to wear loud colors.

"Socks" and "pocketbook" and "dickies" and "petticoat" were crossed off the shopping list.

"Now for the shoe store," Mamma said, "and then we'll go to beauty parlor."

Mary Jane had never in her whole life gotten more than one pair of shoes at a time, but today Mamma let her pick out two — rust-brown loafers and flats that looked like ballet slippers. She was so excited about the flats and Mamma's offer of stockings to go with them for dress-up that she stopped wondering about the "theys." For a while.

At the beauty parlor she squeezed her eyes closed so that she couldn't see the scissors as they traveled around her head. Clutching the arms of the chair, she refused to look at all until Miss Alice, the hairdresser, had trimmed the little fluff in front and brushed away the hairs from the back of her neck. When the haircut was over, Miss Alice turned the chair and held the mirror so that it showed the pony tail. Mary Jane had to admit that it did look nice. And much more grown-up than the braids.

Miss Alice had known Mary Jane since she was a little girl, when she used to come in with Mamma and ride in the chairs until she was dizzy. Only now she called her "Miss Mary Jane" and shook hands as they said good-by.

"Up at the school, if they say mean things to you, just pay them no mind. Just go about your business," she advised.

Mamma frowned at Miss Alice, but she didn't say a word. In the car, riding home, she kept going over her list, making sure they hadn't forgotten anything. Mary Jane didn't say a word either. She was just plain weary, from the fluff on her forehead to the tips of her brand-new shoes.

After they carried all the packages up the stairs and spread them out on Lou Ellen's bed, Mamma looked them over approvingly.

"Least they won't be able to say you're not well dressed," she sighed.

"They" again. It gave Mary Jane a queer feeling in the pit of her stomach. Not a stomach-ache really, but a fluttery, butterfly-wings sort of feeling. As if something was going to happen. Only then Gwen telephoned and Peggy came over to see her new room and her new clothes, and the fluttery feeling went away.

It won't hurt a bit

5

Saturday morning while Mamma went off to market Daddy took Mary Jane to the dentist and the doctor. "It won't hurt a bit," the dentist promised, and it didn't, although he filled two cavities.

The doctor didn't hurt either. He told her to say "ah" and listened to her chest and weighed and measured her. When he was all done he squeezed the muscles in her arm.

"Strong as an ox," he announced. "This girl of yours, she ought to be able to handle things up at the school if they give her a hard time."

He was joking, of course, but Daddy didn't seem to like it. Neither did Mary Jane. She was getting a little bit tired of people talking about Wilson.

There had even been an article in the morning paper. "Six Negro children," it said, "will be the first of their race to enter a previously all-white school in High Ridge on Monday. They are enrolled in Woodrow Wilson High School, which has junior and senior high divisions in the same building."

Mary Jane cut it out carefully to put in the collection of things she was saving for her children, a collection that included second-grade spelling tests, a baby tooth, and her certificate of graduation from Dunbar. Mamma clipped it too, borrowing a paper from the lady next door, so that she could send it on to Lou Ellen.

Of course Lou Ellen knew all about Wilson already. When Mary Jane came home from the doctor's there was a package on the hall table, a package postmarked "Philadelphia" where Lou Ellen's hospital was. Inside the brown paper wrapping Mary Jane found a silk scarf of pale, pale blue. Last year her big sister had sent her red bows for her braids, this year a blue scarf to tie around her pony tail. Trust Lou Ellen to know!

Mary Jane ran upstairs to her new dressing table. She sat there for a long time, looking in the mirror and fooling with the scarf until she'd gotten it just right. Then she fluffed out

the curls on her forehead with a comb, pleased
with the way she looked.

This whole business — the new clothes and
the present from Lou Ellen and the things the
hairdresser and the doctor had said — reminded
her of when she was six and had her tonsils out.
For days ahead of time everyone was particu-
larly nice to her. Mamma fixed her favorite
foods and Daddy bought her a new doll, and
even Mamma's sisters came over with toys.
Afterward, when her throat hurt, they let her
eat ice cream and no vegetables and watch television until real late at night.

The fuss people were making now, they acted
as if going to Wilson was as bad as having
tonsils out. "Only it's not," she told Gwen after
lunch, when they sat down on the porch to
talk. "Sure there'll be a few kids who'll be
mean, it's talked about so much in their homes.
But there were mean kids at Dunbar, too. You
know that. And after the first days, when I get
used to it, it'll be all right."

" 'Spect so." Gwen nodded. "Only I'm glad
I'm not you. I mean, it's scary enough going to
Douglass, just starting high school with those
big kids and algebra and all."

"Nothing to be scared about," said Mary Jane, feeling brave.

"Mmm." Gwen was concentrating. "Mamma says she'd worry something awful if I was going to Wilson. She says she doesn't know how your mother can stand it."

"Mothers always have to have something to worry about," Mary Jane pointed out. "Mine didn't like it one bit either when Lou Ellen went North to nursing school. And the first time Daddy let James drive the car at night, she wouldn't even go to bed until he came home."

"Mmm," Gwen repeated. "Wonder if we'll be like that. When we're mothers."

"Probably," Mary Jane sighed. "I mean, when you get old, something just makes you worry, I guess."

Talking about mothers-are-all-alike helped to quiet the butterfly wings in Mary Jane's stomach. Especially when Mamma invited Gwen to stay for supper and afterward Daddy took them to the drive-in, where they saw a neat cowboy movie.

Sunday school the next morning was all right too. When she came home the house was full of roast-lamb-mint-sauce smells *and* uncles and aunts, each with a present for Mary Jane. Not toys like when she had her tonsils out, but a ball-point pen and cuff links for the new blue shirt and a schoolbag from Aunt Ruth with millions of compartments and pockets. When she thanked her for the bag, Aunt Ruth said something surprising.

"It's me who ought to thank you. What you're doing will make it easier for my Jimmy and the others when they come along."

Mary Jane had never thought like that about going to high school. She was going to Wilson because it was a better school and she wanted to go. But Aunt Ruth made her feel special and important, as if she were an explorer or inventor or something. She was so pleased with herself and everybody else that she didn't grumble after dinner when Mamma asked her to take Jimmy to the playground while the ladies cleaned up and the men sat on the porch to smoke their cigars. So pleased that she pushed Jimmy in the swing about a billion times until her arms ached and Aunt Ruth came to call for him.

When the shadows of the houses grew long and skinny, she walked home. Slowly, because she was thinking about what to wear tomorrow and because that tonsils-coming-out, butterfly-wings feeling was starting up again.

At the supper table she was still trying to decide between the gray skirt and the navy blue and wondering what Mamma would say if she wore her flats to school, when she realized that Daddy was talking to her.

"Mary Jane" — he'd had to say it twice — "Mr. Jackson called before. He and Fred'll be here first thing in the morning."

"Whatever for?"

"We're going to carry you two to school." He sounded offhanded, but Mary Jane was so surprised that she dropped her fork on the floor and had to go to the kitchen to get a clean one.

Daddy always said, "God gave children legs to walk with, not for climbing into cars." Daddy never, never drove her anyplace unless it was miles away. And Wilson wasn't miles away— only five blocks. That was one of the reasons she'd wanted to go there—because it was nearer than Douglass.

Was this more "they" stuff? "They always carry their children to school. . . . You'll look terrible if you walk. . . ."? Only it couldn't be. "They" didn't drive their children to Wilson. Everyone walked there. She'd seen them walking and swinging their books and shouting to their friends, and so had Daddy, plenty of times.

The butterfly wings were beating so fast now that she could scarcely repeat, "Whatever for?"

"Chickadee." Daddy reached over to pat her hand. "While you were on the farm — there's been talk this summer — some people don't want colored going to Wilson High. Tomorrow — well, they might try to stop you. Mr. Jackson, Reverend Coleman, and I saw the police chief yesterday. He said we'd get protection, all we need. Said he doesn't want any trouble, and I believe him. But still — "

Mary Jane watched Mamma fiddling with her spoon, fiddling with her water glass. All grown-ups were worriers, she reminded herself. But suppose this time they were right. Suppose this time there really was something to worry about.

"Chickadee," Daddy continued, "if you wanted to change your mind and go to Douglass, there's nobody who'd fault you. Nobody at all. They'd understand."

Mary Jane shook her head, fighting to catch her breath, to keep back tears. Thinking about Aunt Ruth, and Grampa, who worked so hard to get his schooling, and Red Anne. "I'll go to

Wilson," she managed to say, and nothing more.

Suddenly she wasn't hungry for dessert. Suddenly she was in a great hurry to go upstairs and put out her things for school. To go to her room and close the door and cry.

Only she was too big for tears. Instead of crying, she laid out her things for the morning the way Mamma liked her to do. Looking in the closet, she picked the gray skirt instead of the blue, because the hoop petticoat made her feel princessy and she wouldn't have to remember to hold her stomach in. Then a white blouse and gray knee socks and the loafers with shiny pennies under the flaps, pennies that Uncle Ben had given her that morning.

After that, she fixed her pocketbook. Wallet first, with the pictures of Lou Ellen and James and Grampa and her week's allowance. Comb, mirror, handkerchief, and even a fingernail file.

Last came the schoolbag. Pencils with needle-sharp points, the new ball-point pen, and an eraser that Daddy had brought from his office, a round one with a brush on the end for sweeping away the crumbs. The bag looked empty still, but tomorrow when she came home it would be bulging with books and notes and homework assignments.

Tomorrow. Long after Mamma had come in to check over her clothes and Daddy had said, "Jacksons'll be here at eight, so don't be a sleepyhead, hear?" she sat on her bed, wondering if she'd forgotten anything. Long after they'd kissed her good night, she watched the street light shining through her new drapes and thought about how it would be at Wilson High.

Heads up, eyes front

6

Mʀ. Jᴀᴄᴋꜱᴏɴ and Fred arrived at the Douglases' while Mary Jane was still eating breakfast. Tall Mr. Jackson making polite talk with Daddy while she spooned up her cereal, and Fred looking stiff and uncomfortable in a new suit and freshly shined shoes. Mary Jane almost wanted to giggle, to tell them all that it wouldn't hurt a bit. But she couldn't, because there was a lump in her throat, as if her tonsils had grown back.

Mamma had little frown lines on her forehead as she smoothed the lapels of Mary Jane's new blazer and straightened the bow on her pony tail and asked if she'd remembered to take a handkerchief.

"Now you be good and don't fret your teachers," she said. "Hear?"

It was the same thing she said every year on

the first day of school. The same thing she used to tell Lou Ellen and James when they were little. Only people who knew Mamma well, like Mary Jane and Daddy, could have said there was anything different about her good-by kiss that showed this wasn't any ordinary first school day.

She stood on the porch, waving to them as they drove off. Mary Jane watched her through the back window of the car until she was only a blur. Fred, who had grown about a mile over the summer, was talking about basketball. He talked goals and fouls and dribbles steadily until Daddy parked the car across the street from school. Then Fred stopped — right in the middle of a sentence.

Mary Jane looked out to see what had made Fred stop talking. The fluttery feeling traveled from her stomach to her chest to her throat, and she clutched her schoolbag with a perspiring hand.

"Man!" Fred whistled through his teeth.

Because across the street, in front of Wilson, there was a row of green and white police cars. And behind the cars there were millions of people. Men and women and children sitting on the low stone wall, swarming over the big lawn and crowding the broad limestone steps. Men and women and children shouting and talking until Daddy and Mr. Jackson and Fred and Mary Jane got out of the car, then putting their voices together for a thundering "Boo-o-o!"

For a moment Mary Jane thought about Curly following her to school and how frightened he'd be by the noise. Then she stopped thinking about anything at all. With Daddy and Mr. Jackson on the outside and Fred and Mary Jane in the middle like a sandwich, the four of them marched across the street.

On the school sidewalk, two policemen joined them. The policemen went first, clearing a path through the crowd, leading the way. It was as if they were marching in a parade.

Heads up. Eyes front. One-two-three-four.

Only instead of drums to keep time to there were screams.

A man, angry. "Go back to Africa!"

Mary Jane turned her head, trying to see who it was. What did he mean?

A woman, high-pitched — could it have been a woman? "Pull her black curls out!"

Mary Jane's scalp tingled as if someone were tugging at it. Automatically her hand jerked up toward her forehead, toward the little fluff she'd combed so carefully at her new dressing table that morning. Then Daddy caught her hand, squeezing it in his own.

Heads up. Eyes front. Eyes on the broad blue backs of the policemen.

They were on the steps now, the white steps that led to the open school door. The crowd, not people, but a crazy Thing of faces and open mouths, was behind them, roaring in their ears. The Thing moved closer, closer, until it seemed as if it were about to pounce. Mary Jane stifled a scream, and one of the policemen turned and shouted.

"Stand still. Move back!'"

The Thing stood still, stepped back, turned into people again. In a way, that was worse, because the people were yelling at *her*, at Mary Jane Douglas, beloved daughter of Mamma and Daddy, baby sister of Lou Ellen and James. Mary Jane, who'd never had anything bad happen to her in her life, except to her tonsils, and even then the doctor didn't mean to hurt. They couldn't be screaming at her — but they were.

Daddy squeezed her hand again. Heads up. Eyes front. They were on the landing now, close to the door. A group of boys were chant-

ing, for all the world as if they were at a football game:

> "Two-four-six-eight
> We ain't gonna integrate."

Two-four-six-eight. The four of them marched
through the door and all the way down the corridor to the principal's office keeping time to the
rhythm of the chant.

While they waited to meet Mrs. Davis,
Daddy let go of her hand to give her a quick
little hug. She looked up at him, her eyes round,
black, startled. He looked down at her, straight-
ening the bow on her pony tail, not neatly the
way Mamma would do, but clumsily, like Dad.
Mary Jane put down her schoolbag and straightened it all over again, as if fixing her bow was
the most important thing in the whole world
just then.

"Boy, that was rough," Fred whispered. "Look
at my hand." When he held out his hand, it
was trembling.

"Are you all right?" Daddy asked anxiously.
"Should I take you home?"

Mary Jane shook her head. After the noise
outside it was so quiet in the corridor that her

ears buzzed. It was hard to speak around the lump in her throat. "I'm all right," she gulped. "You can go now."

But Daddy stayed until Mrs. Davis said "Hello" to all of them and introduced them to the other Negro children, three boys and a girl, who were entering the upper grades. When the warning bell rang, Daddy kissed her good-by and Mr. Jackson kissed Fred, who looked embarrassed but pleased just the same. After that it was definitely time for parents to leave and school to begin.

"Junior High Assembly," Mrs. Davis explained as she led them along winding corridors to the auditorium. "This is where you'll get your assignments to your home rooms."

In the big auditorium Mary Jane and Fred sat alone. Alone in the midst of a room full of boys and girls. Alone, as if they were on a desert island in the middle of the ocean.

Mrs. Davis gave a welcoming speech, saying how glad she was to greet all the new people and that she hoped everyone had had a restful summer so that they could buckle down to some good hard work this term. It was a nice speech. Mary Jane had heard Mrs. Buckley give one like it at Dunbar every fall.

After Mrs. Davis' talk, another teacher stood up to read the home-room assignments. She called boys and girls up to the front of the room, one after the other, to get their cards.

The A's, the B's, the C's. Fred looked down sympathetically as the teacher began on the D's. For a moment Mary Jane thought he was going to pat her hand. Only then he remembered that he was a boy and she was a girl and that patting hands just wasn't done, in school or out, first day or last, when you were twelve.

"Mary Jane Douglas." She shivered a little, even though she was still wearing her blazer. Slowly she stood up and walked down the aisle to the front of the room. Head up. Eyes front.

The room was so quiet that she could hear her own footsteps tapping on the floor, her new loafers with the good-luck pennies in them. Until, from somewhere behind her, there was a muffled chorus:

> "We don't want her
> You can have her.
> She's too black for me."

Mary Jane flushed, faltered, kept on walking. Her cheeks were burning as Mrs. Davis jumped up from her seat on the stage and sternly rapped for order.

"Disgraceful . . . no more of that . . . rude . . . won't permit . . ."

Words. Words that Mary Jane scarcely heard as she took her assignment card and walked back to her seat. Head up, eyes front, not listening, not seeing anything. Not even reading the card until Fred came back with his and they compared them. He was in home room 127, she in room 124. Her home-room teacher was Miss Rousseau, the card said.

After all the assignments had been given out and the junior high had pledged allegiance and sung "Oh, say can you see," the boys and girls shuffled through the auditorium doors to the crisscross of corridors beyond. Everyone seemed to know where to go except Fred and Mary Jane. They stood there looking uncertainly at each other, when something surprising happened. At least Mary Jane *thought* it happened. Puzzling over it later, she wasn't sure that it hadn't been a dream.

A girl came up to them, a little girl with bright red cheeks and pale blond hair, and said that she was sorry about the crowd outside. "Can I help you find your way?" she asked. "My sister used to go here, so I know where the rooms are, sort of. It's awfully confusing if you don't."

Instead of answering, they showed her their cards. She led them up a flight of stairs and down a hall to their home rooms. Then she disappeared without even saying "Good-by."

Room 124 was pleasant and sunny, with high windows and movable desks and a green blackboard behind the teacher's chair. Not much different from the classrooms at Dunbar except for the color of the blackboard, and the desks which were brand-new.

Even Miss Rousseau looked like the Dunbar teachers. Ageless, the way teachers always seemed to be, not exactly pretty, but not ugly either. Like the Dunbar teachers, except that Miss Rousseau's skin was fair instead of brown and she talked with a funny sort of accent. She rolled her *r*'s and did things with her *th*'s in a way that Mary Jane had never heard before.

"Good morning." She smiled as Mary Jane hesitated in the doorway, not sure of what to do next.

A bell rang and Miss Rousseau started to assign seats. Alphabetical order again, which put Douglas in the second row, with a window on one side and a girl named Duncan on the other.

Only the girl named Duncan didn't sit down. Instead she marched up to the teacher's desk and loudly announced, "My mother said I wasn't to sit by *her*."

Miss Rousseau lifted her eyebrows. "In my class," she answered, "pupils sit where they are assigned." Calmly she continued to read out the names.

The girl named Duncan started to leave the room, then thought better of it. Without looking at Mary Jane, she slid her desk over until it was almost touching the one at her right. It stayed there until Miss Rousseau finished with her seating list.

"Now, Darlene." The teacher's voice was calm. "You can put your desk back in place."

Mumbling under her breath, Darlene obeyed. Through the entire period, however, she kept her head turned toward the door. If she *had* to sit next to Mary Jane, at least she wasn't going to look at her. For a crazy moment Mary Jane felt like giggling. Darlene was going to have an awful stiff neck by the end of the term.

The next minutes were busy ones. Miss Rousseau gave out schedule cards and locker num-

bers and explained about periods and bells and
lunch and gym and not being late and bringing a note to the nurse if you were sick. Then
the whole class trooped out to the hall to find
their lockers and practice their combinations.

The combinations worked like the locks on
safes. Two turns to the right. Stop at 27. One
turn to the left. Stop at 14. Then right again
until the lock clicked open when you reached 7.
Mary Jane twirled and stopped and twirled and
stopped until she knew her combination by
heart. After she hung up her blazer on the hook
inside the locker she went back to her home
room.

There was another bell and still another, and
regular classes began. Today was only a half
day, so classes meant learning your teachers'
names and getting your seat and your books.
For first period Mary Jane stayed right where
she was, alongside Darlene, because their class
was French and Miss Rousseau taught it.

Miss Rousseau not only taught French, she
was French, she told the class. Which explained
the funny accent. At any other time Mary Jane,
who had never met a person before who didn't
come from North Carolina or Kentucky or

Tennessee, would have been interested in someone from Paris, France, who said "ze" when
she meant "the." But not today when her head
ached and the back of her neck felt sore and
she couldn't swallow the lump in her throat no
matter how hard she tried.

After French and more bells came English
and more bells, then Arithmetic, History, and
Science. Only History was called Social Studies
now, and Arithmetic was Math. All of the classrooms looked like her home room, except Science, which had tables instead of desks and a
sink in the back of the room, and Social Studies,
which had Fred.

Mary Jane had never realized before how
much she liked Fred until she saw his friendly,
dark face when she entered the Social Studies
room. While people were still finding their
seats, he leaned forward to whisper in her ear.

"Already I've been kicked in the shins and
had my books knocked out of my arm. Score,
Wilson two, Jackson nothing. This keeps up,
I'll get a complex or something. I'll begin to
think they don't like me," he chuckled.

"Who did it?" Mary Jane's lips framed the
words as the teacher called the class to order.

Fred shrugged his shoulders, the smile gone from his face. "Seems like all of them."

Mary Jane chewed her underlip as she copied the homework assignment from the board. "Columbus Finds a New World, pages 3–11." The next bell would mean Science, and then school would be over for the day. The bell after the next one would mean going outside to face that howling, hating crowd. Maybe, she thought, they wouldn't be there. Maybe they had forgotten and gone away. But after she'd taken her blazer from her locker and found Fred and then Daddy in the noisy vestibule, she knew that the crowd was still outside, still waiting.

Down the steps and across the lawn she walked, with the policemen leading and the voices screaming. Mean, hate-filled voices screeching in her ears. She blinked at the white light from a photographer's flash gun. She ducked when a stick glanced off her shoulder. But she wasn't what you'd really call hurt. She was still putting one foot in front of the other and squeezing Daddy's hand and trying not to listen to the roar of the crowd.

One-two-three-four, and they had crossed the street. One-two-three-four, and they were in the car. With the doors closed and the windows rolled up to shut out the noise.

It was the end of Mary Jane's first day in junior high.

Your great bravery

7

Driving home in the car with everybody sighing, sort of, and not talking, Mary Jane remembered her tonsils again. It had been like this after the operation when she left the hospital with Daddy. She'd been shaky still, kind of dopey from the medicine the doctor had given her to stop the hurt in her throat. And at home Mamma had been waiting on the front steps with a worried frown on her face.

Only now she was twelve instead of six and Mamma wasn't going to put her to bed with ice cream and coloring books and a promise that the pain would stop after a while. Now she was twelve and maybe this special going-to-an-integrated-school pain would never stop. Unless she stopped going to the school.

But she put all thought of leaving Wilson

out of her mind, because Mamma was hugging
her as if she'd been away for a year instead of
a few hours — and Mamma was starting to cry.
All morning she had listened to radio reports
about school. All morning she had pictures in
her mind of Mary Jane being chased down the
halls, bloody and maybe dying. Mamma practically never cried, and the sight of her red-
rimmed eyes made Mary Jane say that everything was all right, just fine, over and over
again.

Before they had finished lunch, reporters
started ringing the doorbell. Ladies with note-
books and men with cameras, asking how old
she was and what she wanted to be when she
grew up and how she had felt that morning in
school. Along with the reporters came phone
calls. Lou Ellen, all the way from Philadelphia,
almost crying like Mamma, and James from
law school, and Grampa and the aunts. By the
time she said to each of them, "It's all right,"
she had begun to believe it herself.

Grampa was the only one who didn't ask
about school. Instead, he talked about Curly
and Sophie and the chickens, until she wished
it were summer and she were back on the farm.

Then he chuckled his slow, deep chuckle and said, "Guess what I was doing when the man on the radio told about that mob outside Wilson this morning?"

Mary Jane couldn't guess. To tell the truth, she was too tired even to try.

"Praying for rain, a regular cloudburst." As he chuckled again, Mary Jane pictured the people outside of school with the rain falling into their open mouths. She burst out laughing.

She was still giggling when Daddy took the receiver from her hand to find out what the joke was about. Standing next to the phone, she listened to his conversation.

"You'd have been real proud of her, Pa. Not a bit upset. She walked up those steps and into that school this morning with her head in the air. As if she were sniffing pies in Heaven."

"Not a bit upset." Mary Jane wandered into the kitchen to find something to nibble on. Chewing on a carrot stick, she thought about what Daddy had said. He hadn't even noticed that she was scared. He was real proud of her, and so was Grampa. Pretty soon she got to feeling real proud of herself — and not a bit upset. Even when the other kind of phone call started.

The first time she picked up the receiver and
it wasn't someone she knew, a man's voice said,
"You take that black girl out of the white school
or we'll kill her." There were others, women as
well as men, calling mean names and threat-
ening to blow up the house and Daddy's office.
After that first call Daddy wouldn't let her
answer the phone any more. By suppertime he
had taken the receiver off the hook.

"Just talk," he said. "People talk like that,
they don't do anything. But there's no need us
listening to it."

When the paper boy tossed the *Evening
Chronicle* on the porch, Mary Jane discovered
that she was front-page news. There she was,
more important even than the President today,
with a picture of her walking up the school
steps. Right behind her was a white girl, her
mouth all twisted, face ugly with hate. Not
just any strange white girl, either, but the girl
named Duncan, Darlene Duncan, who sat next
to her in home room and in French.

She stared at the picture for a long time,
trying to understand it. Gosh, Darlene didn't
even know her. How could she make a face
like that? Of course, that's what Grampa had

said. "They just don't know you." Maybe even Darlene—when she knew her, would change her mind.

Borrowing the scissors from her mother's sewing box, Mary Jane cut out the picture and put it in the bottom drawer of her desk, along with the baby tooth and the spelling papers and the graduation certificate from Dunbar. What in the world would her children think when they saw that picture? She'd have to tell them the whole story, the way Grampa told her about Red Anne.

Feeling proud of herself and pleased with all the excitement and with everyone at home acting so nice, she pushed out of her mind any thought of not going back to Wilson. Even when she was lying in bed at night and could still hear the women screaming and the men calling names.

The excitement didn't stop with that first day. Reporters kept coming and newspapers printed Mamma's picture and Daddy's and Fred's, newspapers all over the country. One man even wanted her to go to New York to be on a television show. Mary Jane's eyes lit up, but Mamma said of course not, she was supposed to be a student, not a star on television.

Then letters began to arrive, great big stacks of them every morning. A few were awful, calling her a "black baboon" and worse, words she didn't always understand. But most of the people who wrote said nice things and some sent little presents, handkerchiefs and dollar bills.

The letters came from every place you could think of, New York and Chicago and Los Angeles, and then faraway places like Paris and Berlin and Stockholm, Sweden. Weeks after school opened, the postman delivered one addressed "Miss Mary Jane Douglas, High Ridge, U.S.A." It had come all the way from Tokyo.

Mary Jane gave the stamps to Fred for his collection and stuck the letter from Japan in the mirror of her dressing table where she could read it, mornings, when she brushed her hair.

"Dear Miss Mary Jane," the letter said. "I am a schoolgirl in Tokyo, reading of your great bravery. From the top of my heart I wish luck come to you. Please excuse English. Your friend, Fuji Yanase."

"It's all right." Mary Jane repeated it to the

reporters and the people who wrote letters and to Mamma and Aunt Ruth and Gwen and Peggy and Daddy. "It's all right," she kept on saying. Even when it wasn't.

Sniffing pies in Heaven

8

THE SECOND DAY at Wilson was a little better than the first. Now that she knew what to expect, Mary Jane concentrated on not listening to the shouts and screams. She marched up the steps with her head high, as if she were sniffing pies in Heaven. She marched up the steps like Joan of Arc and Red Anne and the Mary Jane who had said she was going to school to get an education, not to socialize.

Fred helped too. When the boys on the landing chanted:

> "Two-four-six-eight
> We ain't gonna integrate,"

Fred squared his shoulders and recited back:

> "Eight-six-four-two
> Ten to one, we bet you do."

Pretty soon Mary Jane joined in with him and they walked through the door and up to their home rooms, saying it in chorus, without breaking step except when they stopped to tell their fathers good-by.

Mary Jane kept on holding up her head and not listening all through home-room period and right into the middle of French. Only then she was so busy not listening that she couldn't answer when Miss Rousseau popped a question at her. Then she flushed and stammered until she could hear Darlene tittering. Then she didn't feel brave any more.

After French, other things went wrong. She took a left turn in the corridor when she should have turned right. She went down a flight of stairs when she should have gone up. By the time she reached English she was breathless and late and scared.

Wilson was so big, with so many stairways and halls and a new wing and an old one, that she was afraid she'd never learn her way around. Everyone else knew where to go. Everyone else walked in twosomes and three-somes, with their friends.

Lunch time was the scariest of all. When the first lunch bell rang, the seventh- and

eighth-graders burst out of their classrooms.
They slid across the shiny terrazzo floors, swinging books and pocketbooks and yelling at the
tops of their lungs. It made Mary Jane think
of a herd of cattle stampeding, running down
anything that got in its way.

She flattened herself against a wall until
everyone had passed, hoping that she'd be able
to find Fred. When he came along, they got on
the cafeteria line together. They slid their trays
around the steam tables, choosing what they
wanted to eat and paying the lady at the cashier's desk. Then they set out down the long
center aisle to look for seats.

The cafeteria was an enormous room, as big
as a football field, with row after row of long
tables. Boys sitting at some tables, girls at others, and everyone shouting "Hi" and "Sit here"
— only not to them.

Nobody paid attention to them at the steam
tables or the cashier's desk, but when they
walked down the aisle with their loaded trays
there was a sudden hush. The big noisy room
grew quiet as Mary Jane put down her sandwich and milk and Fred his hot plate and two
desserts at a table near the door. It was so
quiet that you could hear the scraping of a

chair when the girl seated nearest Mary Jane got up and walked away. Quiet and then buzzing with sound, with everyone whispering and poking his neighbor to look.

Fred shook his head, meaning go-on-and-eat. He started right in on his hamburgers, but Mary Jane didn't feel hungry. She ate slowly, carefully, nibbling at her sandwich and wiping her mouth with her napkin after each sip of milk. She could almost hear Mamma saying, "Mind your manners. They'll be watching you."

They certainly were watching. After a few minutes of everybody staring and nobody at their table saying a word, Mary Jane whispered to Fred, "I feel as if I had two heads or something, the way they look at us."

"Likely they've never seen Negroes eating before," Fred said, right out loud. "Likely they think we'll pick up our meat in our paws and lick our plates."

Fred certainly was a help. One or two people at their table heard what he said and stopped staring. And by the time Mary Jane had watched him plow through his hamburgers and his two desserts she found her courage coming back. Of course it was that they didn't know any better, that they thought colored people were different. Once they got to know her, everything would be all right.

She hardly fussed when a boy blew the paper cover off his milk straw and it hit her on the cheek. At Dunbar, kids were always blowing the covers off their straws — when the teacher wasn't looking — and hitting kids with them. There it didn't mean a thing. Maybe someday she'd get so used to Wilson she'd blow her straw cover at a kid too. These things just took time.

Time passed, and Mary Jane kept on going from brave to scared to brave again and from not listening to listening. She learned her way around the high school corridors and which stairs to take to English and to Gym. She bought red and white Wilson covers for all of her schoolbooks and she saved her allowance until she had two dollars for a G.O. card so that she could go to all the school games. She was even getting used to the sudden hush when she sat down at a cafeteria table or walked into the noisy, crowded lavatory. Not liking it, of course, but getting used to it.

Time passed, and every morning there were fewer and fewer people standing in front of the school. Until finally there was only one police car at the curb and Daddy and Mr. Jackson said it would be all right, she and Fred could go to school alone.

At home the phone calls stopped — even the mean ones — and there was only a trickle of letters from faraway places. At home all the excitement had died down. The worry lines were fading from Mamma's forehead and she began to scold Mary Jane about picking up her room and helping with the dishes and making sure her homework was finished before she turned on the television. Daddy, working hard on a big case, was too tired to take her to the drive-in on Saturday night or to remember to pat her on the shoulder and tell her she was his big, brave girl.

It was as if the tonsils were out, the sore throat healed, and everything the way it had been other years. Only everything wasn't the way it had been other years.

Mornings, Fred called for her and the two of them walked to school together. The grown-ups were gone, but there was always a handful of boys and girls lounging on the school steps. Waiting to shout, "Why don't you go to your own school?" Waiting to call names and threaten to hurt them.

Mary Jane listened now and heard the things
they said. She wasn't sniffing pies in Heaven
any more. She was paying close attention when
a boy bigger than Fred held up a water pistol
and pointed it straight at her.

"It's full of acid," he called. "If you go into
school, I'll shoot."

Of course it wasn't acid, only water that
splashed Fred's pants and Mary Jane's socks.
But all during French she shivered, not because
her legs felt damp, but because it might have
been acid after all. All during French she stared
at Darlene, trying to figure out what made Darlene hate her so. Because she was still sniffing
and sniggering and moving her desk away when
Miss Rousseau wasn't watching.

Darlene wasn't the only one. On the way to
lunch, people stepped on her heels or bumped
into her, hard, in the corridor. And there was
one boy in study hall who kept kicking the
back of her seat.

When she complained about these things at
home, Mamma looked unhappy. She tried to
comfort her, saying, "Could be an accident," or
"That's just school life." But even Mamma
didn't say it was an accident the time she forgot
to close her locker door and someone spilled

red ink over her notebook and the composition she'd just recopied for English.

At first the people at school were blurred, the way they are when you go to the eye doctor and he puts drops in your eyes. At first everyone looked alike, but after a while she was able to tell them apart. She could recognize the red-headed boy with the water pistol when he jabbed her with his elbow in the hall. She knew the tall girl with the pony tail who was good in English and the captain of the seventh-grade volleyball team. And the little girl in Science with pale blond hair and bangs who wore baby dresses and looked too young to be in high school.

Not all of them were mean. There were one or two girls who nodded when they passed her in the corridor. In classes some of them asked her for the homework assignment if they had forgotten to copy it. There was even one girl, Sharon, who walked with her from Math to the cafeteria two days running. She acted so friendly that Mary Jane thought she might invite her to sit at her table at lunch.

Until the third day, when Sharon said, "Mary Jane, you can tell me. Confidentially, weren't you born in New York? And aren't they paying you to come here to get Negroes into Wilson?"

Mary Jane widened her eyes, not understanding the question. "New York? Pay me? I've lived in High Ridge all my life. I was born here and — "

Sharon sighed. Mary Jane could see that she was disappointed. "Darn it," she said. "I had a bet with Elizabeth that you came from the North. The way you talk — " She went away, shaking her head.

Fred laughed when Mary Jane told him about it over lunch. "Don't you get it? You don't talk the way she thinks Negroes talk. You're supposed to say, 'Dishere chile sho' nuff bawn in de Souf,' like Aunt Jemima or Old Black Joe or somebody."

"They've got this picture of a Negro in their minds," Grampa had said. And she had answered, so sure of herself then, "They'll learn. I'll be like some ambassador from a foreign country."

Only it wasn't easy being a foreign ambassador to people like Sharon who seemed nice but didn't really want to find out what you were like. It wasn't easy being a foreign ambassador when your only friend in school was

Fred and he was busier and busier with basketball practice.

At Dunbar, Mary Jane had been busy too, acting in plays and on the Student Council and writing stories for *Dunbar Doings*. But here when she went to sign up for after-school things like cheerleading, the captain of the squad, one of the senior girls, stared at her, embarrassed. And then blurted out, "I'm afraid you wouldn't do. I mean, you wouldn't match — your color wouldn't match ours. You do see that, don't you? I mean, it's nothing personal."

Mary Jane saw lots of things. Like in Gym, when she was the last one to be picked for volleyball every single period, even though there were other girls who were worse players. Or when they had folk dancing instead of volleyball and no one wanted to be her partner.

Even the gym teacher was uncomfortable then, not knowing what to do until Sally, the little girl from Science, came up and asked would she dance. Mary Jane wanted to say "No," but she couldn't, not with the teacher standing right there listening.

Sally's cheeks were scarlet and her hand shook as she took hold of Mary Jane's. She looked as if she were going to cry. Mary Jane felt like crying too, but she spread her lips in her best imitation of a smile and danced one turn around the room.

Before the second number was called, she murmured to Sally that her ankle hurt and left the floor. People didn't have to dance with her when they didn't want to, just because they felt sorry for her or something. To tell the truth, Mary Jane was feeling sorry enough for herself.

The day of the first frost

9

TIME PASSED and the leaves fell from the trees
and Mamma took the winter clothes out of
moth balls and announced that Mary Jane
needed a new coat. One morning when she
looked out of her bedroom window, the grass
was silver-gray instead of green. The first frost
meant an end to Grampa's flowers and tomatoes, meant snugging up the barn and the
chicken coop so that the animals would be
good and warm, when winter came.

Mary Jane didn't want to think of Grampa.
He had tried to warn about Wilson and she
hadn't believed him. He had said she'd get to
feeling that the whole world was against her.
And it was. Maybe not the whole wide world,
because of people in France and Sweden and
Japan who wrote her letters. But the part of
the world that mattered most to Mary Jane —

the world of High Ridge and Wilson High — was certainly against her.

Even Mamma and Daddy. When she was little it seemed as if they could fix up anything that went wrong. Trouble in school or fights with her friends, they always knew what to do. But now, at Wilson, it was different. If she talked about the kids in school, they said, "Pay them no mind," or "That's ignorance. You ought to feel sorry for a person who acts like that." And lately when she came home scuffling up the steps and snapping at their questions, they sighed and said, "Maybe she'd best transfer to Douglass after all." As if that was any help.

Even Gwen and Peggy and Laura. Gwen and Mary Jane had been best friends since first grade, with Peggy and Laura joining them in second. They'd been the Four Musketeers and the Amazons and the Bluebirds, besides being in the same Brownie troop and then Scouts. They'd sewn dolls' clothes and played stickball and baked cookies and had slumber parties to talk about boys.

Only now Gwen and Peggy and Laura were working for their curved bars in the Scout troop at Douglass. They sang Douglass songs and talked about clubs and teachers and boys she didn't know. When she phoned them now, asking them to sleep over on a Saturday, they were practically always busy. Even when she did see them, it wasn't the same. It was as if they thought that she thought she was better than they, by going to Wilson. It was as if they'd be glad if she quit and transferred to Douglass.

Even Fred. It wasn't fair to say that Fred was against her, because he wasn't. But Fred was the tallest boy in the whole seventh grade, and those hands of his were just made to curve around a basketball and aim it at a hoop with loving care. It seemed as if the color of a person's skin didn't matter so much to many of the boys. Only a very small minority complained when the coach put Fred on the class team and said he'd make junior varsity if he kept on. So Fred stayed after school to practice in the gym and Mary Jane walked home alone.

Yesterday in the cafeteria Fred had stammered and acted uncomfortable. "Some of the fellows," he said, "they asked me to eat with them. I told them I didn't know. Told them I'd see. I thought, maybe, if you weren't with me, the girls would ask you. I mean, if we keep on sitting together all the time — "

Mary Jane had assured him that it would be all right, just fine, if he ate with the boys. So now even Fred had deserted her.

Walking home by herself wasn't too bad. Some days she'd cut out of a side door and run along a back street. Run real fast, feeling free as a jay bird, with classes over and no one looking at her funny — or not looking at her at all.

Walking home by herself wasn't too bad, but eating lunch alone in that great big cafeteria — Just thinking about it brought out goosepimples on Mary Jane's arms. Maybe that was why she had gone from brave to scared to brave to mad.

These days, everything Mamma said irritated her and even Daddy wasn't much better. He acted as if she were still a child, funning and saying silly rhymes like:

> *"What is the matter with Mary Jane?*
> *She hasn't a care. She hasn't a pain.*
> *But her chin's dragging down to her*
> *knees again."*

That used to work when she was little, but

not now, when he tried joking her out of a bad mood she ran upstairs and slammed the door of her room.

Looking in the mirror of her dressing table, she wondered why they couldn't see that she wasn't a baby any more. Her face felt stiff and frozen a good part of the time, and she had discovered that if she let her eyelids droop and looked up at people through her lashes, they couldn't tell at all what she was thinking.

Even her voice was different. Not changing like Fred's. His voice went from deep and rumbling to high and squeaky when he got excited. Hers was flat and toneless, to match her stiff face. A voice that said "Yes, ma'am," and "No, ma'am," when she didn't feel the least bit polite inside. She was also finding out about another voice, a screaming, angry one that started deep in her throat and came up with all sorts of things that she didn't even know she was thinking.

Like on the morning of the first frost when she and Fred were walking into school. That same redheaded boy was standing on the steps, the one with the water pistol, and two or three others. Muttering as they always did, words like "pickaninny" and "jigger" out of the corners of their mouths. Only instead of not listening and paying no mind, Mary Jane screeched at them suddenly. "Shut your mouth! Hush up and die!" and worse, things she'd never said before in her whole life.

She was almost as surprised as Fred. "Rise above it," he cautioned in a good-humored growl as they walked down the hall. "Don't let it get you down."

It was all very well for him to say, "Rise above it." Him and his basketball players. Mary Jane's hand was shaking as she turned the knob on her locker. She had to take a deep breath and start all over again before she could work the combination.

In home room, Darlene was sprawled with her legs stretched out, fixing to trip her if she didn't look sharp. Every other morning Mary Jane detoured around the legs. But today she pushed them aside with the toe of her loafer and marched straight ahead.

Darlene hollered "Ouch" good and loud. Miss Rousseau looked up but the bell rang and she started reading the daily bulletin. Announcements about a meeting of the Science Club, tryouts for the girls' basketball team, choir practice.

"Nothing for me," Mary Jane grunted to herself. "My skin wouldn't match any of their old clubs."

Opening up her French book, she began to go over her homework. *J'aime, tu aimes, il aime. Cher ami, je t'aime.* Her frown deepened. No wonder she couldn't learn this stuff. I love, you love, he loves. Dear friend, I love you. How did you say "hate"? They never taught you things like that.

Turning to the vocabulary at the back of the book, she hunted up new words. Hate, *détester, abhorrer.* Enemy, *ennemi.* With her tongue curled over her lip, she copied them in her notebook, then made them into sentences. *Je déteste mon ennemi. J'abhorre mon ennemi.* I hate my enemy.

Not quite satisfied, she erased the *mon* and started over again. *Je déteste mes ennemis.* I hate my enemies. From now on that was the way it was going to be. No more *j'aime* and *cher ami* for her.

Her pencil clattered on her desk as she noticed Miss Rousseau standing behind her. She tried putting her hand over her notebook, but she could see from the teacher's lifted eyebrows that it was too late.

"I would like to talk to you, Mary Jane," Miss Rousseau said. "Will you stay for a moment after class?"

Mary Jane's heart thudded as she dropped her eyelids and said, "Yes, ma'am." French was her hardest subject, and if Miss Rousseau was going to be mad at her —

But Miss Rousseau wasn't mad. After the others had trooped out of the room she chewed her lower lip, thinking. "Your other teachers tell me you're doing very well in their classes, that you'll make the honor roll if you can bring up your French. I thought — it being first period — you're upset when you come in——"

Mary Jane waited, face frozen, eyes half closed. What was she trying to say?

"I thought — if you'd like to come in after school — just for a little while — I could go over some of it with you to bring up your mark."

Now it was Miss Rousseau's turn to wait as Mary Jane considered the offer, then rejected it. Stay after school? Give Miss Rousseau a chance to ask questions, feel sorry for her maybe?

"No, thank you, ma'am. I mean, my mother expects me home. I mean, I'll work a little harder on the French, that's all."

Then she had to excuse herself and run so that she wouldn't be late for English. She was still trying to figure out why Miss Rousseau hadn't mentioned *mes ennemis,* when she heard Miss Morgan, the English teacher, say her name.

"The best composition today was Mary Jane's. I want her to stand up and read it to the class."

Why did she have to go and do that? Mary Jane's cheeks were hot and her hands sticky as she took the paper from the teacher. "My Favorite Pet." Clearing her throat, she began to read about Curly. Read as fast as she could, because there was a snort behind her and she heard someone say, "Mary Jane, the pig's best friend," and "I told you she lives in a pigsty."

Miss Morgan heard it too. Her face turned a dark red as she scolded Clarence, the boy who'd said it. "If you wrote as good compositions as Mary Jane's you'd have something to snort about. See me after school."

Of course that didn't make Mary Jane feel any better and it made Clarence so angry that he shoved her in the corridor, accidentally on purpose, and she shoved him back, not even pretending that it was an accident.

Math was easy, just review of problems she'd had last year. Like going to the grocery store

to buy five pounds of potatoes at twelve cents
a pound and you had to multiply five by twelve.
She got all the problems right, but the teacher
didn't call on her and she didn't bother to raise
her hand. Because by that time she was beginning to worry about lunch.

Eating alone, with everyone staring and no
one to talk to. No one to joke with so that
you could laugh and pretend you didn't care.

"But I *don't* care," Mary Jane told herself.
"They hate me and I hate them. *Je déteste mes
ennemis.*"

Saying it in French made it sound better
than in English. Fiercer. After lunch she'd look
up "I don't care" in the vocabulary and write
that down too. But why wait? If she brought
her French book to the cafeteria with her she
could look up all kinds of things to say while
everybody was watching.

Eating her sandwich with the book propped
against her container of milk, she didn't see
Fred wave or notice that Sally — Science and
folk-dancing Sally — paused at her table as if
she wanted to speak to her.

I don't care. *Je m'en moque.* Leave me alone.
Laissez moi seule. Shut up. *Assez!*

"*Je m'en moque.*" She said it out loud, almost

giggling at the startled expressions of the girls at the table. They didn't know her, and now they didn't know what she was talking about either. *"Laissez moi seule,"* she said as she walked out of the cafeteria with her nose up in the air.

She was opening her locker to put her French book away, when Miss Collins stopped to speak to her. Miss Collins was the music teacher, in charge of the chorus that sang in assembly every Friday. Miss Collins was old and sort of twittery and some of the kids made fun of her.

"Mary Jane, I was wondering" — she hesitated — "why you don't come out for choir?"

Mary Jane wanted to ask, "Whatever for?" but all she said was, "Ma'am?"

"Do you sing alto or soprano? We could use some more altos in the chorus, and then there's the Christmas program. I thought it would be nice. I mean, your people . . ." Her voice trailed off.

Mary Jane was so surprised that she didn't know what to say. In Dunbar the music teacher always told her *not* to sing when they had assemblies. Here Miss Collins was asking "alto or soprano" and inviting her to join the chorus.

"But I can't sing," she protested.

"Come now, let's not be shy," Miss Collins said, getting a bit twittery. "I just know you have a sweet little voice. Don't you sing in your church?"

Mary Jane wrinkled her forehead. How could she *know?* Mary Jane never sang in school. To tell truth, she hadn't sung once since she left the farm. And certainly not in Sunday school, where everyone knew that she couldn't carry a tune.

"But I can't sing," she repeated. "Except flat, I mean."

"I'm sure you're just being modest." Miss Collins shook her head. "All your people have such wonderful voices. I just love your spirituals. Now suppose you come to the music room at three and let me decide where to place you."

For the second time that day Mary Jane found herself saying, "No, thank you, ma'am. I mean, my mother expects me home." Only this time her voice cracked, almost the way Fred's did. Because she suddenly understood what Miss Collins meant.

All "your people," all Negroes have beautiful voices and sing spirituals. Just as all Negroes

say "dishere chile" and "sho' nuff, honey." A
teacher thought that. Not just a girl like Sharon,
but a grown-up teacher! As if the color of your
skin could have anything to do with your voice.
As if she and Daddy and Grampa didn't have
practically the worst voices in the whole state.
Maybe Fred would think Miss Collins was
funny, but she didn't.

She was getting mighty sick of "your people."
Miss Thomas kept saying it to her and Fred in
Social Studies whenever they talked about slav-
ery. The class was up to Eli Whitney and the
cotton gin, and today's lesson showed a picture
of women with bandannas on their heads and
sacks tied to their waists, picking cotton.

Sure enough, as soon as Social Studies started
and they turned to the picture of the slaves,
everybody craned necks to look at her. Probably
thought Mamma wore a bandanna and a sack
tied to her waist and went around all the time
picking cotton. Darn old Eli Whitney and his
cotton gin anyway.

She walked from Social Studies to Science
murmuring, *"Je déteste Eli Whitney."* Science
was the class she liked best. Not just because
Mr. Stiller was young and jolly, although he
was, but because he taught about animals and

plants and microbes and insects and all the things she and Grampa were interested in.

The room was nice too. It was in the old wing of the building and the tables were scarred and worn, not shiny-looking, and the floors were scuffed, the way the floors at Dunbar used to be. All along the window sill there were plants—flowers and beans and ferns and little green water plants in a big aquarium. There were cages with white mice in front of the plants and flat pans with turtles crawling around.

In the back of the room there was a big case filled with things, like in a museum. A hornets' nest and snakeskins and neat fossils and a skeleton labeled "walleyed pike." Whenever she had time before class began she stopped to look over the museum exhibits or to play with the turtles and white mice.

Today Mr. Stiller was talking about conservation, about how some crops take nourishment out of the soil and you have to plant others to put it back again. Mary Jane knew a lot about that because when Grampa was younger he used to travel around, talking to the farmers about planting soybeans instead of tobacco every year.

"Grampa says," Mary Jane volunteered, "that there are little bacteria that grow on the roots of soybeans and put nitrogen back in the soil."

"Grampa says — " For a few minutes Mary Jane forgot about being mad. She forgot about *je m'en moque* and *je déteste*. She was busy waving her hand and quoting Grampa and feeling pleased when Mr. Stiller nodded his head and agreed with them both.

She kept on feeling pleased until the last bell rang and everyone got up to leave. Until the girl walking along the corridor with Darlene loudly asked, "Who's her grampa, anyhow?"

"How do I know?" Darlene smothered a yawn. "Some cotton-picking old darky, I suppose."

Grampa an old darky cotton-picker! All the snubs and shoves and misunderstandings of today and yesterday and last week and the week before were suddenly jumbled together in Mary Jane's head. Without thinking of what she was doing, she swung her schoolbag up in the air and brought it down—hard—on Darlene's shoulder. And then ran—fast—down the corridor, down the stairs, and out of Wilson High.

To the rescue

10

Down the broad steps, across the lawn, past the police car. Only then she stopped. The wind was blowing, piling up the leaves in the street, bringing goose-pimples to her bare arms. She couldn't go home without her blazer or Mamma would scold. She couldn't go home like this, running away from everything. She couldn't face Daddy and Aunt Ruth and Fred and Grampa and tell them she'd quit.

Slowly, rubbing her arms to warm them, she retraced her steps. Slowly, scuffling at the leaves on the path, she walked back to Wilson High.

Miss Rousseau was waiting for her in the vestibule, and so was Darlene. Angry, complaining, triumphant Darlene.

"Mary Jane," Miss Rousseau scolded, "whatever are you thinking of, running out without your jacket in this weather? You'll catch your death."

"She hit me," Darlene shouted. "Right here on my shoulder. She has no right to go to our school."

Miss Rousseau didn't answer Darlene. Instead she led both girls up the stairs to their home room and told them to sit down. "Now," she asked, "what's this all about?"

"She hit me," Darlene repeated. "I wasn't doing a thing, just walking along the corridor to my locker and she hit me. My mother says —"

Miss Rousseau sighed. "Mary Jane?"

Mary Jane didn't answer. What *could* she say? Tell about the redheaded boy on the steps and Darlene's outstretched legs and "your people" and Grampa being —— Miss Rousseau wouldn't care. Nobody cared. Let them go ahead and expel her from Wilson. She didn't care either. Not much, anyway.

"Did you hit her?"

Mary Jane nodded, her face frozen, her eyes studying a joint in the floor. "I hit her," she mumbled.

"It still hurts," Darlene said. "Something awful."

Miss Rousseau sighed again, looking tired. "But why did you hit her? There must have been some reason."

"No reason at all," Darlene insisted. "She just hauled off and hit me with her schoolbag. I couldn't have been more surprised."

No reason. Mary Jane jerked up her head. No reason? After what she said? "She called my grampa an old darky cotton-picker." Her voice was low, as if it hurt even to repeat the words.

Miss Rousseau frowned at Darlene. "Well, maybe I did say something like that," she admitted. "But that's no reason — "

"It was an ugly, unkind thing to say and I want you to apologize for it. And as for you, Mary Jane, you know better than to go around hitting people when you have a grievance. You must apologize too."

Apologize. Say you're sorry.

"Never," Darlene shouted. "I'll tell my mother. She'll tell Mrs. Davis."

Mary Jane studied the floor some more. She *was* sorry, not because she'd hurt Darlene, but because she did know better than to go around hitting people and she was glad that Miss Rousseau understood that she did.

"I apologize," she mumbled without lifting her eyes.

"Now, Darlene" — Miss Rousseau turned toward her — "I'm going to talk to Mrs. Davis too. About the way you try to trip Mary Jane in the mornings and move your desk and the things you say. I had hoped that if I ignored you, you'd stop after a while. But I won't have that kind of behavior in my room any longer."

Darlene's face turned from red to white to red again. She was scared of Mrs. Davis, the way everybody in seventh grade was. In a voice even lower than Mary Jane's, "I apologize," she muttered.

"Very well, girls. You may go now." Miss Rousseau nodded. "And don't let me hear of anything like this happening again."

Darlene scooted out as fast as she could. Mary Jane followed slowly. She wanted to speak to Miss Rousseau, to say something like "thank you," but she couldn't quite bring out the words. Because Miss Rousseau, in spite of being a teacher at Wilson High, didn't seem to be against her. Maybe she hadn't been nice, exactly, but she had certainly been fair.

Outside, with the sun shining and the wind blowing the leaves, she didn't feel cold any

more. Swinging her schoolbag, she started to
run. Not running away from anything or running home because Mamma might worry if
she was late, but because with the sun shining
and the wind blowing her hair back, running
felt good. She ran one block, two blocks, three
blocks, until she was out of breath and had to
slow down to a walk.

A crowd of people from school were standing
at the corner, waiting for the green light. Big
boys mostly, and some girls. Only, she saw as
she drew nearer, they weren't waiting for the
light to change. They were gathered in a circle
with their books under arms and their hands
in their pockets, watching something.

Most days, feeling mad at everybody from
Wilson, Mary Jane would have walked right
on. But today, surprised about Miss Rousseau
and all out of breath from running anyway, she
paused. Weaving her way into the crowd, she
stood on tiptoe to find out what they were
watching.

In the center of the circle a big yellow tomcat
was chasing a ragged half-grown squirrel. The
cat hissed and humped his back while the squirrel tried frantically to escape from the cat's
clawed paws. Flicking his tail, baring his teeth,

the squirrel broke away, only to have the cat pounce on him at last.

Some of the boys cheered. Some of the girls squealed in horror and closed their eyes. But nobody tried to rescue the squirrel. Mary Jane dropped her schoolbag and rushed furiously at the cat. She tugged at the loose fur on his neck and grabbed at his paws until he let go of the squirrel and turned on her. He raked her face with his claws before running away.

The squirrel lay on the sidewalk, too stunned to move. When Mary Jane picked him up, he squeaked feebly and dug his sharp teeth into her thumb.

Ignoring the pain, she cuddled him in her arms as if he were a baby, then buttoned her blazer around him to keep him warm. Through her blouse she could feel his heart beating against her own. At least he's alive, she thought.

The boys and girls were all talking to her now, but she didn't hear them. Shouldering them aside, she headed for home.

"Mary Jane! Hey, Mary Jane!"

She was halfway down the block before she turned to see who was calling. It was Sally, with her hair tumbling over her face as she puffed after Mary Jane.

"You forgot your schoolbag," Sally shouted,
and waved the bag. "How is he? Will he be
all right?"

Mary Jane waited for her to catch up. "Hope
so." She let Sally peep inside the blazer and
stroke the squirrel's head.

"I can look him over better when I get home,
see if any bones are broken."

"Do you know how? I mean, did your grampa
tell you how to fix animal bones and everything?"

Mary Jane nodded, a little bit puffed up because of the respect in Sally's voice. "Not squirrels' bones exactly, but I guess I know what
to do."

They progressed slowly, Sally bumping two
schoolbags against her legs and Mary Jane coo-
ing at the bundle of fur in her arms.

"You're so lucky," Sally sighed. "I mean, getting to live on a farm and all. That's always
been my ambition, living on a farm. I'm crazy
about animals, but my mother won't even let
me keep a dog."

"My mother either," Mary Jane said. "Mine
wouldn't even let me keep a white mouse a
friend of my brother's wanted to give me. Only

a dopey parakeet once that died. My mother just hates pets."

"Mine too." Sally was struck by a sudden thought. "Say, what'll she say about the squirrel? And you? Your face really looks terrible. Does it hurt?"

"Some. Thumb's the worst, where the squirrel bit." Mary Jane held it up so that Sally could see the teeth marks.

"Gee, it's bleeding. Stop and let me put my handkerchief around it. Funny," Sally said, "funny him biting you when you just saved his life."

Mary Jane put her thumb in her mouth to suck away the blood. "You'd bite too if you were hurt that bad," she defended the squirrel. "Probably you'd bite the very first person came along."

"Probably," Sally hastened to agree. "But your mother. Think she'll let you keep him?"

Mary Jane took a deep breath. The closer she came to home, the less sure she felt about Mamma. "She just has to, leastwise till he's well. She *has* to let me keep him."

Walking and talking and stopping to admire the squirrel, they had turned into Mary Jane's block in no time at all and were marching up

Mary Jane's front steps to the porch where Mamma was waiting.

Mamma never used to wait on the porch when Mary Jane went to Dunbar. Now she stood there every day, twirling a lock of hair between her fingers and looking anxiously down the street and then at her watch to see if Mary Jane was late.

Mary Jane thought Mamma didn't understand how hard things were at Wilson. Truth to tell, Mamma understood more than Mary Jane knew. Every night she talked with Daddy about transferring her to Douglass. Every day she paced the porch, fearful that some harm had come to her little girl.

And today, seeing Mary Jane walk up the steps with her hair tousled and her face all scratched and blood on the lapel of her new blazer, she was sure that someone had hurt her. Today, seeing Mary Jane come home like that with a strange girl carrying her schoolbag, Mamma exploded.

"It's happened at last," she moaned. "I told your father it would. Now I hope everyone's satisfied."

She hollered at Mary Jane and Daddy and Aunt Ruth. She hollered at Grampa on the farm and at "they" who were up at the school. None of it made any sense unless you knew about the days and nights and weeks of worry that were enough to make anybody, even a mother, explode when she thought her daughter was hurt.

Only Sally didn't know about the days and nights and weeks of worry. When Mrs. Douglas glared at her and said, "Run along now," in an ice-cold voice, she dropped Mary Jane's schoolbag on the porch. Her blue eyes looked like the round china eyes of a doll as she backed down the steps and ran. Ran without even stopping to say good-by or to tell Mary Jane that she hoped the squirrel would get better.

Mary Jane stamped into the house and ran to the living-room couch. She hadn't cried since school started, not even when she had to squeeze her lids tight shut to keep back the tears. Now she didn't try to keep anything back. She sobbed for every little thing that had happened and howled for every big one. And the more things she remembered, the more tears streamed down her cheeks.

Furry

11

WITH BRIMMING EYES herself, Mamma tried hugs and shoulder-patting and handkerchiefs and wet washcloths. But it seemed as if nothing could stop Mary Jane's wails until the squirrel, shaken up by all the sobbing, poked his head out of her blazer.

"Pfutt, pfutt, pfutt," he scolded.

Mamma jumped back and gasped and started to climb on a chair the way she did at the farm when she saw a mouse. Even with the tears still flowing, Mary Jane just had to laugh.

After that, between giggles and hiccupy sobs that still kept coming, she explained about the cat and the squirrel and Sally, who had acted as if she wanted to be her friend. If she didn't happen to mention about hitting Darlene, well, it was probably because she forgot.

Mamma felt so glad that nothing really had

gone wrong and she felt so bad about her explosion that she went out to the garage and found the old parakeet cage. Before Mary Jane asked even once, she said, "You can keep the squirrel in this for a few days, until he gets better. Only then you have to let him go."

The squirrel looked better already. Patches of fur were missing where the cat had clawed him, and he dragged one of his hind legs across the floor of the cage as if it were broken. But he seemed spry enough otherwise as he waved his tail and studied them with his big bright eyes.

Mary Jane was figuring out how to put a splint on his hurt leg when Mamma started acting like Mamma again. First the scratches on Mary Jane's face had to be washed and the teeth marks on her thumb examined. Then there was a worry over lockjaw and rabies and all manner of infections. After that nothing would do but to telephone the doctor and carry Mary Jane right over to his office. Mary Jane wanted to take the squirrel too, so that the doctor could fix his leg, but Mamma wouldn't hear of it.

The doctor calmed her down. "Hasn't been a report of rabies in High Ridge since I started practicing, and that's a long time," he explained.

He gave Mary Jane a tetanus shot for her
scratches and a Band-Aid for her thumb and
a handful of the wooden sticks he used when
people said "aaah." To make splints for the
squirrel's leg, he suggested.

It wasn't easy, fixing the splints. First time
she tried, the squirrel bit her finger again. "Now
that I've had the tetanus shot," she comforted
Mamma, "nothing can happen to me."

The second time she tried, he climbed out
of the cage and limped across the living room.
Words wouldn't comfort Mamma then. She
ran to the kitchen and closed the door until
Mary Jane promised to wait with the splints
until Daddy came home.

Before Daddy's key turned in the front-door
lock she had named the squirrel Furry and had
practically tamed him. He made all kinds of
noises, chattering and squealing, and even a
bubbly sort of purr, like a cat. Mary Jane fed
him nuts and crackers and pieces of apple and
slices of orange until Mamma said he'd get sick
if he ate anything more.

As soon as the dishes were cleared from the
table, Daddy tied the splints on Furry's hind
leg with gauze bandage while Mary Jane

stroked his head to keep him quiet. He chewed at the splints at first, as if he didn't like them, but after a while he stretched out on the floor of his cage and went to sleep. With his feathery tail wrapped around him like a blanket.

Mamma, who was still feeling ashamed about her explosion, said Mary Jane could take Furry upstairs to her room if she kept him locked in the cage.

"About the little girl, about Sally," she added. "If I wrote her a note saying I was upset and I'm sorry, you could give it to her in school tomorrow."

"Probably won't do any good." Mary Jane shook her head. "I mean, it was the squirrel she was interested in anyway, not me." And then, because she didn't want to let on—even to herself—how she felt about Sally, she poked her nose up in the air and announced, "*Je m'en moque.*"

"What's that you're saying?" Daddy asked.

"*Je m'en moque.* French for 'I don't care.' I don't care about anything except Furry—and you, of course," she added politely.

In the morning while Mamma fixed breakfast, Mary Jane cleaned Furry's cage and gave him a piece of bread to chew on. He sat up on his haunches, holding the bread in his front paws as if they were hands. Even Mamma had to admit that he did look — well, cute, and not a bit like a mouse. Mary Jane left her with a list of instructions about food and fresh water before she ran outside to meet Fred.

Thinking about Furry, she hardly noticed the boys on the school steps or Darlene's pouty face. And at lunch time, instead of looking up new words in her French vocabulary, she went into the library for a book on squirrels. While she ate, she read all about them. About red squirrels and gray ones and how their teeth keep growing like people's fingernails and how they line their nests with moss and grass.

It was going to be hard to find moss and grass in High Ridge this time of year. As soon as Social Studies was over, she hurried into the Science room to consult with Mr. Stiller. He was interested, remembering about a squirrel he had kept for a pet when he was a boy.

"You can use ordinary drugstore cotton instead of moss," he advised her, "although if he's warm I doubt he'll try nest-making. The important thing to watch is his diet. Don't give him all soft, starchy stuff like bread. He needs nuts and acorns, too, for those teeth of his.

Probably you could collect enough acorns in the park to keep him happy for quite some time. You know, in that grove of oak trees near the pond——"

Mr. Stiller stopped, looking uncomfortable, looking as if he wished he'd never thought of acorns. Because "the park" meant Calhoun Park, north a little way from the high school. And Mary Jane didn't know the grove of oak trees near the pond because Negro children weren't allowed in Calhoun Park. They had playgrounds near their homes and one swimming pool in summer, but they couldn't go Calhoun Park. They couldn't walk on the paths or play under the trees or even collect acorns for a squirrel that was hurt and needed them.

Sally, listening to the conversation, didn't notice Mr. Stiller's face. "I know where you mean," she broke the silence. "I know where there's tons of acorns in the park. You want to come with me after school, Mary Jane? I'll show you a fabulous place to find them."

Mary Jane frowned. She'd been wondering what to say to Sally after yesterday and Mamma and all, but if Sally was going to be so dumb —

"No, thanks," she answered in her cool, dead

voice. "I mean, I'm busy today after school."

As the bell rang for class Sally made her way to her seat with a hurt expression on her face. Mary Jane felt sorry. After all, Sally had meant to be nice, offering to find the acorns. Only she oughtn't to act dopey. Mary Jane was tired of being a foreign ambassador.

Today was lab day for the Science class, Mr. Stiller explained. Instead of going over the lesson in the book, they were going to learn how to use microscopes and look at little things mounted on slides.

"Pair off," he said. "You'll have to take turns, two to each microscope."

There it went again. Mary Jane had hardly put Calhoun Park out of her mind when she had to start thinking about a Science partner. Who could she pair off with? Not any of the people sitting next to her, not Darlene or her friends certainly. She twisted around in her seat to look over the others, wishing that Fred had Science this period instead of Shop.

In the row behind, Sally caught her eye, then turned beet-red. Well, did she want to be her partner or didn't she? Somebody had to say something, and when practically everyone else was paired off Mr. Stiller said it for them.

"Sally — Mary Jane — suppose you two work together. Sally, get the microscope from the closet and, Mary Jane, you pick out a slide to look at."

Mary Jane took a slide labeled "Clay" and slid it under the lens of the microscope Sally was setting up on the table. While Sally turned the mirror to catch light from the window, Mary Jane squinted into the eyepiece. She couldn't see a thing.

"Not like that," Sally advised. "Better keep both your eyes open. Let me show you." Then she blushed.

Mary Jane had never seen anyone in the whole wide world who blushed as much as Sally.

"Didn't mean to sound bossy," Sally apologized as she took over the eyepiece. "But my father — he's a doctor — he showed me how to work it."

Everyone else was calling, "Mr. Stiller, help us!" and "Is this right, Mr. Stiller?" while Sally and Mary Jane were turning the focusing knobs and looking at particles of clay and sand and then a fly's wing and after that a slide labeled "Amoeba," which they thought was a tiny animal but weren't quite sure.

It wasn't until the bell rang that Sally asked, "How's the squirrel?" and Mary Jane answered, "He's okay." Then, because Sally had been so nice, teaching her how to work the microscope and all, she reported on Furry's broken leg and the splints and the way he ate, sitting back on his haunches.

Talking squirrel talk took them to their lockers and down the corridor and right out to the sidewalk. They were all the way to the South Street corner, where Sally had to turn for home, and Mary Jane was saying, "Even Mamma's getting to like him a little," when she remembered about yesterday's scene on the porch. She could tell that Sally remembered too, because those cheeks of hers were turning crimson again.

Mary Jane took a deep breath and without looking at Sally began to talk quickly. "Mamma says to tell you she's sorry about what she said. I mean, she doesn't usually explode like that. In fact, hardly ever."

"My mother says" — Sally was staring at the sidewalk too — "it's like you said about Furry yesterday. 'You'd bite too if you were hurt bad.' Not that your mother bit, I mean, but blowing up like that could happen to anyone if they're worried and all, Mother says. And I think —"

But Sally, about to melt from embarrassment, couldn't bring herself to say what she thought. With a mumbled "G'bye" she scooted around the corner as fast as she could go.

Mary Jane stood stock-still, watching her, before she headed for home. Sally's mother knew about Mamma worrying and her feeling hurt. At least that sounded like what Sally was trying to say. That meant — well, that someone else in High Ridge wasn't against her. Only — well, Mary Jane wasn't quite sure. Sally and her mother would take some thinking about.

Sally and her parents

12

THE AFTERNOON sped by. Furry was so comical to watch that Mary Jane would have forgotten all about homework if Mamma hadn't reminded her. When she fed him a chunk of bread he sat up — really stood on his hind legs — with his ears perked and his tail twitching, until he'd eaten most of it. Then he gravely buried the rest under the cotton she'd given him for his nest. By the time Mamma called, "Set the table, sugar. I hear Dad's car going into the garage," he was taking crackers right out of her hand. She liked the feeling of his nails on her palm, sharp as little thorns.

When supper was over, she carried Furry up the stairs to her room. After closing her bedroom door carefully, she opened the door of his cage and let him out. Of course it was disobeying, but a squirrel needed exercise, more than he could get in a little old parakeet cage. And Mamma and Daddy were so busy watching their favorite television program that they wouldn't even know.

Furry sat on her desk with his front paws pressed against the white fur of his chest, as if he were going to make a speech. Then he dropped down on all fours and with a flick of his bushy tail began to explore. When he ran, the splints on his leg went "clump-clump-clump" on the surface of the desk, and he looked back with such a human, surprised expression on his face that Mary Jane burst out laughing.

Afraid that Mamma might hear the "clump-clump," she moved Furry from the desk to the bed. "Much better," his bright black eyes seemed to say as he scurried across the spread and scrabbled up the drape that covered the window. Dragging his splinted leg, he couldn't climb very fast, but he climbed and jumped down and climbed up again until Mary Jane reached into the pocket of her blouse for a nut. One nut, two nuts, and he was sitting on her shoulder, helping himself with his long-fingered paws.

Nuzzling her face in his soft, warm fur, she

sighed. If only she had someone to show him off to, to share him with. Someone who really liked squirrels. Someone like Sally.

When her clock warned that it was close to the end of Mamma's television program she put Furry back in his cage. Sitting down at her dressing table, she puzzled about Sally and her mother. Could they really be different from other people in High Ridge? Could they really not be against her?

Her eye caught the letter from the Japanese schoolgirl that was still sticking in her mirror. Maybe that was it. Maybe Sally and her mother didn't come from the South. Maybe they came from some faraway place — not Japan, but Philadelphia or New York — where folks didn't always have wrong ideas about Negroes. Tomorrow in Science she'd ask Sally, sort of casual-like, where she came from.

She remembered the question as soon as she walked into the Science room the next afternoon. But before she could look for Sally, Sally came up to her.

"Mary Jane — " Sally began.

"Sally — " Mary Jane said.

"You say first."

"No, you."

Each girl was being so polite, telling the other to go first, that it looked as if neither would get anything said before class. At last Sally held out a paper bag. "For Furry," she explained. At the exact same moment Mary Jane asked, not casual-like at all, "Where were you born?"

Sally's eyebrows came together in a puzzled frown. "High Ridge, of course. In Women's Hospital, where my father works. But why — ?"

Mary Jane was glad that the bell saved her from having to answer Sally's question. All she could think of was Sharon, who had asked, "Where were you born?" because she had this crazy picture of colored people in her mind. Now she had been practically as silly as Sharon.

The paper bag rattled and felt bumpy on her lap. While Mr. Stiller talked she peeped inside. Acorns — big fat shiny brown acorns that Sally must have gathered in Calhoun Park yesterday afternoon. Turning to look back, she framed "Thank you" with her lips and Sally smiled.

Maybe this was what Grampa meant when he said she'd learn too. And that the whole world wasn't against her. Because now she could count some people on her side. Not an

awful lot, maybe, but Miss Rousseau and Mr.
Stiller and Sally, she felt pretty sure.

Mary Jane waited at the classroom door
when the last bell rang so that she could tell
Sally how Furry climbed up the drape and balanced on her shoulder and reached into her
pocket for nuts.

"I just wish you could see him," she said.

"Me too. I mean, I wish I could," Sally answered.

They were at their lockers, putting on their
jackets and not looking at each other. Because
if Mary Jane wanted Sally to see Furry and
Sally wanted to see him, well then, what was
stopping them both? All Mary Jane had to say
was "Want to come?" All Sally had to say was
"Can I?" But neither of them did. All the way
to the South Street corner they made busy talk
about Furry and acorns and a test that Mr.
Stiller was going to give them tomorrow.

During supper that night Mary Jane was
so quiet that Daddy said, "Penny for your
thoughts." Said it twice, in fact, before she
heard him. She held out her hand, and after
he'd put a penny in it and she had grinned at
the joke, she turned serious again.

"Do you know Dr. Green? Works at the Women's Hospital?"

"Heard of him." Daddy nodded. "Folks say he's a pretty nice fellow. Good doctor, too. Why? Are you thinking of getting sick?"

"He's Sally's father. You know" — Mary Jane nodded toward Mamma — "the girl who came home with me the other day."

"Well, what do you know." Mamma was pleased. "I've met her mother. A long time ago when Lou Ann was at Douglass and I was head of the PTA. Mrs. Green was head of the Wilson PTA, and we had a joint meeting. Celebrating Lincoln's Birthday, if I remember correctly. We sat together on the platform and she was real polite. Not funny the way some are."

"Some." That was another way Mamma had of saying "they." And "they," Mary Jane had discovered by now, meant "white people." She thought for a moment before asking, "You mean, they're not all against us?"

"Of course not," Daddy scolded. "You know better than that. Look at those letters you got."

"Letters don't count," Mary Jane argued. "I mean right here in High Ridge."

"Even in High Ridge," Daddy said. "There have always been people, like at that PTA meeting. They came to our churches and we went to theirs. It's just the last year or two, since school integration started, that feelings have been running high. I guess there are some who would like to speak, but they're afraid. And of course some do speak."

"Mrs. Green," Mamma added. "She speaks. Don't you remember last year, time of the school board election? There was this one man, Mr. Courtney, and white people were down on him because they said he was for integration. Mrs. Green wrote a letter to the paper saying people should obey the law and go along with the Supreme Court decision."

"And did they?" Mary Jane asked. Last year when she was only eleven she hadn't been paying much attention to elections and newspapers and the Supreme Court.

"Well, yes." Daddy laughed. "Else what would you and Fred be doing at Wilson? The school board went along with the Court, only lots of people don't like what they did."

Mary Jane made a face. Didn't anybody need to be telling her *that*. "Mrs. Green — do you suppose she'd care — I mean, if I asked Sally — she's interested in Furry — all kinds of animals, in fact — "

"I suppose by all that floundering around like a fish on the riverbank you mean should you invite Sally to come see Furry," Daddy interrupted. "I don't rightly know what to advise. From what I hear, Dr. and Mrs. Green are fine people. But whether they'd like their daughter associating with a Negro girl outside the school, that's something else again."

Mamma slowly shook her head. " 'Tisn't what they like. It's the whole community. Their friends and the doctor's patients — there are sure to be plenty who'd object."

Mary Jane's face clouded over. Object to what? As if it was anybody's business but Sally's and her own. As soon as Mamma told about meeting Mrs. Green and her letter to the paper, she'd been picturing herself saying "Want to come?" when she and Sally stood at their lockers tomorrow, and hearing Sally answer "Sure." Now it was all spoiled.

"I'd take it easy yet a while." Daddy was talking. "Times are moving fast, but you can't change feelings that have been built up in people, not in one day. If Sally acts friendly to you in school, that's just fine. But wait a little before asking her home."

Mary Jane pushed back her chair and began

to clear the table, banging down the dishes as she carried them to the counter in the kitchen. She didn't know whether she felt madder at the Greens or at Mamma and Daddy. It was easy for them to say "Wait." They were old and, besides, they had their friends. While she had only Furry.

Of course, having Furry wasn't half bad. He could do a lot to cheer her up. He chittered with joy when she came into the living room after supper, reaching through the bars of the cage to hunt in her pocket for food. While Mamma was busy with the dishes, Mary Jane took him upstairs to play. He could climb nimbly now. Even with the splints, he could scramble all the way to the top of the drape and make a flying leap back to the bed.

Having Furry wasn't half bad. He could do a lot to cheer up Mary Jane. Until he had to go and spoil it all.

He's got to go

13

IT WAS ONE of those rainy, blue-Monday kind
of days. Mary Jane came home from school
wet all over, with her hair plastered down on
her head and her feet leaving a muddy trail
up the front steps. Mamma was waiting in the
living room instead of on the porch. Mamma
didn't look worried. She was just good and mad.

While Mary Jane was leaning against the
doorjamb taking off her wet shoes, Mamma
started in. "Your squirrel has got to go," she
said. "Nutshells all over the rug, cracker crumbs
on the couch, that's bad enough. But today — "

She broke off to fetch a towel to dry Mary
Jane's hair. For a few minutes it was hard to
find out exactly what Furry had done. But when
Mary Jane heard the whole story her heart
sank right down to her wet socks.

While Mamma was at the store in the morning, Furry had somehow opened his cage door and roamed through the house. He had knocked over a vase of flowers in the living room, broken a glass in the kitchen, and torn a pair of brand-new stockings that were lying on Mamma's bureau upstairs.

"Where is he now?" Mary Jane hardly dared to ask.

"In the bathroom, causing goodness only knows what kind of trouble," Mamma scolded. "I took a broom and shooed him in there."

With her shoes in her hand, Mary Jane ran up the stairs, taking them two at a time. Furry was sitting in the sink with a mischievous expression on his face. As soon as he saw Mary Jane he scampered over to show her the tube of toothpaste that he'd found. The tube of toothpaste that he'd chewed open and squeezed all over Mamma's clean room. There were white toothpaste worms on the floor and the bathtub and the shower curtain and on Furry's soft gray fur.

Mary Jane wanted to laugh, except that it wasn't funny. Not when she thought about what Mamma had said. She carried him down to his cage with a solemn face.

"I'll clean up everything. I really, truly will,"

she promised. "And I'll pay for the glass and the stockings. You can start taking it out of my allowance right this Saturday."

Mamma shook her head. "I said you could keep him till he got well. Any beast causes the trouble he did, he's *well*. He belongs outdoors, not in a civilized house."

She said lots more about Furry being a wild animal and her home not being a zoo. None of it sounded very hopeful, but Mary Jane begged and pleaded and argued all the same. She showed Mamma how she could put an extra piece of wire on the cage door so that Furry wouldn't be able to open it again. She pointed out that his broken leg wasn't all healed and indignantly asked, now that it was practically winter, how Mamma thought he could keep himself warm and well fed.

It didn't do any good, of course. Once Mamma had made up her mind, she was awfully stubborn about changing it. "He'll manage," she calmly announced. "He'll manage as squirrels have managed for millions of years. Soon as you've put on dry clothes, you take him outside to the yard or the playground and let him go. Hear?"

"In this rain?" Mary Jane raged. "You want

him to catch pneumonia? You want to murder
him?"

The rain and Mary Jane's woebegone face
softened Mamma a little. But only a little. Furry
could stay, she agreed, until tomorrow after
school. Then he absolutely, positively had to
go. When Mamma talked like that there was
no use arguing. And even Daddy, when he
came home, wouldn't go against her decision.

Mary Jane stormed and slammed doors and
sulked upstairs in her room. In the morning the
sun shining through her curtains didn't make
her feel the least little bit better. She wouldn't
even say good-by to Mamma, and when Fred
started talking about the junior varsity she was
scarcely polite. He was going to play on the
team next week and he wanted her to come
cheer for him. She grunted something that
could have been "yes" or could have been
"no." Truth to tell, she doubted she would ever
cheer for anything again.

She was beyond answering back the boys on
the school steps, and when someone in the corridor shoved her she didn't bother to look up
to see who it was. At lunch she sat alone,
staring into space, without even trying to hide
behind a book. She had just about decided to

run away to Grampa's, to break open her piggy bank and take the bus and Furry to the farm, when Sally stopped at her table.

"Something wrong?" she asked.

Mary Jane looked up with a scowl. For a moment she hated Sally, hated her pale, silky hair and her doll-blue eyes and her short, baby dress. Hated Sally and her mother and the whole wide world.

But when Sally, blushing, hesitating, said, "Can — can I help?" she pushed away her half-eaten sandwich and followed her to the corridor. After all, at least Sally would understand about the dangers to Furry from cats and cold weather. At least Sally would understand how very, very much Mary Jane would miss her pet.

"But you can't let him go," Sally groaned after she had heard the story. "We'll just have to think of something."

"We?" What did she mean, "we"? This was Mary Jane's squirrel and Mary Jane's problem. "I'm going to run away." She tossed her head. "Take Furry and go to Grampa's. And never never come back to High Ridge, even when I'm grown."

"But you can't run away," Sally protested.

"I mean, it's not just Furry. People would think — "

She stopped, but Mary Jane knew what she meant. People would think that she was running away from Wilson High. Well, so she was —running away from the boys on the steps and the girls in the lunchroom and Darlene and Sharon and Miss Collins—and from her very own mother, who didn't appreciate squirrels.

"Can too run away," she answered crossly.

"But I mean, my mother says you've been so brave and — " Sally's cheeks were crimson.

"Your mother — she does?" Mary Jane was interested in the idea. She hadn't thought about being brave for weeks and weeks, not since the last letter had come from abroad. But then, being brave wasn't going to take care of Furry. "Your mother" — she took a deep breath — "you don't suppose she'd let you keep Furry?"

"No use even asking, 'cause I know just what she'd say." Sally sighed. "She means to be nice and all, I guess, but she just hates animals. Same as yours."

Mary Jane sighed too. It was getting close to the end of lunch period. If Sally was going to come up with an idea, she'd better hurry.

"Somebody who likes animals." Sally was

thinking out loud. "At the hospital they have white mice in the lab — "

White mice! Both girls snapped their fingers at the same moment. Mr. Stiller kept white mice in the Science room. If he liked mice, he'd certainly like Furry, who was bigger and smarter and a hundred times more fun.

He was sitting at his desk, marking tests, when they dashed into the room. Putting down his red pencil, he looked up at the two anxious faces, at the snapping brown eyes and the round blue ones. He listened carefully as they told him about squirrels and mothers and how Furry wouldn't be any trouble, really not a bit.

"We'll bring his food — "

" — and clean his cage — "

" — if only — "

" — please —"

When they paused for breath, he slowly nodded his head. "Won't hurt to try, see how it works out," he said. "Be good for the classes to watch. Weekends are a problem, but since the janitor feeds the mice then, I guess he wouldn't object to taking on your squirrel."

Mary Jane felt like shouting "Hurrah," but all she said was, "Today? Could I bring him right

after school? My mother says I positively have
to get rid of him today."

"Today'll be fine," Mr. Stiller agreed. "Only
scoot right home and fetch him, because I've
an appointment at four. And be sure not to forget food for his supper."

Two more classes, and then Mary Jane and
Sally slid down the corridor to their lockers.
Grabbing their jackets, they ran for the door.
Was Sally going to come home with her, to help
bring Furry back to school? Mary Jane won-
dered about it all the way down the steps, but
she didn't ask. At the corner of South Street,
Sally turned off, calling, "See you later." Mary
Jane waved an airy good-by, as if she hadn't
expected anything else.

At home she was far too busy to think about
Sally. Bursting into the house with a "Hi" for
Mamma, who was sitting in the living room
with Aunt Ruth, she started grabbing nuts from
the cupboard and bread from the breadbox
and an orange from the refrigerator. Pretty
soon Mamma and Aunt Ruth were grabbing
things too and stuffing them into paper bags
and telling her to take it easy, because Mr.
Stiller would surely wait. When they saw how

excited she was, Aunt Ruth offered to carry her and Furry back to school in her car.

In no time at all Aunt Ruth parked at the front entrance of Wilson and helped Mary Jane unload and then load up again. When she left, Mary Jane was holding Furry's cage in her hand and the bags of food tucked under both arms.

"Hey, wait for me!" It was Sally, backing out of a car with her arms wrapped around an enormous burlap sack.

"Birdseed," she panted as they staggered up the steps. "The squirrels always steal it from our bird feeder, so I figured Furry would like it."

She didn't explain, perhaps because she was too breathless to talk, that she had taken all of her savings and an advance on next week's allowance to buy the sack of seed. She didn't explain, and it never occurred to Mary Jane to ask.

Mr. Stiller laughed when they puffed into his room with their bundles. One of Mary Jane's bags burst, scattering crackers and nuts all over the floor. "I said supper," he protested, "not a year's supply for an elephant."

They put Furry on the window sill, where he could look at the plants and the mice and the turtles and doze in the afternoon sun. Then, because Mr. Stiller said he still had a few minutes, Mary Jane opened the cage to let the squirrel explore. He leaped to her shoulder, poking his paw into her pocket for a nut.

Sally squealed with delight and begged for a turn to hold him. She gave him birdseed and talked baby-squirrel talk into his little oval ear until Mr. Stiller began to look at his watch and noisily clear his throat.

Pretty soon Miss Rousseau walked into the room. Even though she was all dressed up in a nice blue suit, she wasn't afraid to pet Furry and feed him seed from Sally's sack. She told them about a park in Paris where the squirrels were tame and would come right up to the benches to beg for nuts.

After Mr. Stiller had put on his topcoat and closed his brief case and said, "Let's leave now, girls," for perhaps the tenth time, Mary Jane put Furry back in his cage. Walking out of the building with Sally and the two teachers, she wondered how she could ever have thought of running away. Wilson High was pretty nice after all. She guessed that she was getting used to it at last, now that she and Furry had made some friends.

Mascot of Wilson High

14

It was funny how quickly everybody at school found out about Furry. When Mary Jane went to visit him at lunch time, the Science room was crowded with sightseers. Mr. Stiller didn't want anyone to handle the squirrel except Mary Jane and Sally, but boys and girls, even from Senior High, brought acorns and crackers and begged to feed him through the bars of the cage.

It wasn't long before Furry was as spoiled and sassy as Curly. And almost as fat. He chattered and scolded the livelong day until Mr. Stiller, half laughing, half angry, threatened to put him in the closet so that he could have some quiet during classes.

Mary Jane could almost hear Grampa singing in his rumbling bass:

"It made the children laugh and play
To see a squirrel at school."

It certainly made the children act nicer. Girls who had never spoken to her before came up and asked where she'd found Furry and how she had tamed him and what they could bring for him to eat. In French class when Miss Rousseau called on her for the word "squirrel" and she said *écureuil* everybody laughed and clapped hands. Not really everybody, because Darlene didn't clap and neither did some of her crowd.

Darlene looked disgusted when *Wilson Times*, the junior high paper, printed an article suggesting that Furry be made the school mascot in place of the old teddy bear the cheerleaders brought to basketball games. She crumpled the paper into a ball and tossed it into the home-room wastebasket, all the while muttering about "zookeepers" and "wild-animal smells."

Mary Jane's face didn't feel the least bit frozen and stiff as she listened to Darlene. She didn't care what Darlene said now that she and Furry had made some friends. She really could pay them no mind now — Darlene and the ones who yanked her pony tail in the corridor and the redheaded boy with the water pistol who still stood on the school steps.

Wilson Times gave her a good idea. After classes in the afternoon she went to a store near home and bought red and white ribbons to decorate Furry's cage. As soon as Science was over the next day, she carried Furry down the back stairs to the boys' gym to see the junior varsity game.

Last week or the week before, even when Fred invited her, she wasn't sure about going to a basketball game. She wasn't sure how people would behave toward her. But today, with Furry and his cage all dressed up in the school colors, she didn't worry a bit.

Boys and girls laughed when they saw the red bow around Furry's neck, and some of them moved over to make room for her on a bench down front. It was Fred's first varsity game, and he scored three times, with Mary Jane rooting for him and Furry sayin "Phutt, phutt," and losing his bow in the excitement.

Sally walked upstairs with her after the game, keeping her company while she took Furry back to the Science-room window sill. They chattered away, wondering if it was time to take off the squirrel's splints, and Furry chattered happily too, as if he knew that they were talking about him.

Mary Jane was putting fresh water in the cage when Mr. Stiller came over to the window. "Hello, you two," he said, and then, "I'm afraid that I have bad news."

Bad news. Mary Jane stood stock-still, waiting for him to explain.

"Some of the mothers object to Furry. They're afraid of his biting people, carrying disease. Mrs. Davis says — Well, we can't keep him here any more. He'll have to go."

Mary Jane's eyelids drooped and she looked up at Mr. Stiller through curving lashes. "Yes, sir," she answered in her flat, toneless voice.

She understood right away that Mr. Stiller meant what he said, but Sally argued, sure that she could get him to change his mind. She pointed out how friendly Furry was and how people wanted him for a mascot and how he never bit at all, not since the very first day when he'd been hurt.

Mr. Stiller wrinkled up his forehead. "Rabies," he interrupted Sally. "Some of the mothers are afraid of rabies, and I have to admit there's always a possibility — "

"That's silly," Sally said, and then blushed because that wasn't the proper way to talk to a teacher. "My mother said rabies too when I first told her about Furry. But Dad said chances were about a million to one that he'd have them, because the health department cleaned up rabies in High Ridge simply ages ago. I mean, an animal doesn't just get rabies out of the air. He has to catch it from some other animal. So if there isn't any rabies in High Ridge, where'd Furry get it from?"

Sally paused to catch her breath, sure that she'd given Mr. Stiller an argument that he couldn't answer. But the teacher shook his head.

"The chances may be a million to one, but so long as there's that one chance, we can't take it. Don't you see?"

Mary Jane saw. She buried her face deep in squirrel fur, wishing Sally would be quiet.

"I know what we could do" — Sally had an idea — "have Furry vaccinated against rabies, the way they do with dogs. Then everybody'll know he couldn't get them."

Mr. Stiller, looking just as sorry as he could be, told Sally that her idea wouldn't work. "So long as there's a chance of even a fleabite, the school can't take the responsibility. It may be all right with your mother, but some other mothers, three or four of them, came to see Mrs. Davis — "

Mary Jane felt cold from her forehead all the way down to the tips of her toes. There was no sense keeping on talking. She turned her back on Mr. Stiller and Sally to fasten the catch on Furry's cage.

"These mothers" — Sally still pursued the subject — "you could phone them to explain about vaccination and how everybody likes having Furry in school. Maybe, if they're in the PTA, they're people my mother knows. Maybe she'd phone them."

Mr. Stiller had a funny expression on his face. His voice sounded strange, almost as if he were angry. "I'm afraid calling them wouldn't do any good. You see, these women — well, they're from the Mothers' League. People like Mrs. Duncan and — "

Mary Jane didn't wait to hear any more. Now that she was going to high school and reading the newspapers, she knew that the Mothers' League was not the PTA. The Mothers' League was organized by the women who stood in front of school on opening day and yelled, "Pull her black curls out." Why couldn't Sally get it through her dopey head that the Mothers' League was not objecting to a little gray squirrel but to a little brown girl?

A home for Furry

15

MARY JANE was halfway down the block with Furry's cage in one hand and her schoolbag in the other before Sally caught up with her.

"Mr. Stiller says we could leave Furry in the Science room till tomorrow, while we try to find a home for him," she announced.

Mary Jane shook her head. Her throat felt tight and she didn't trust herself to speak .

"Darn that mean old Mothers' League." Sally kicked a pebble across the sidewalk. "Whatever are we going to do now?"

Mary Jane scowled. There was Sally with that "we" stuff again. It was *her* squirrel that Darlene's mother objected to. *Her* squirrel who had no home. *Her* squirrel who was never going to be the mascot of Wilson High's basketball team. A single tear rolled down her cheek as she looked at the bedraggled ribbons on the cage.

Petending not to notice, Sally went right on talking. "We could try my father — the hospital. If they took Furry, we couldn't see him so often, but he'd have a good home. And the sick people would like him, I bet. Should I phone and ask?"

Mary Jane nodded. She really didn't think much of the idea, but she didn't have a better one to propose. While Sally went across the street to call her father, Mary Jane sat down on the low stone wall that bordered the school property. Sat down with her head bent and Furry's cage between her feet.

People from school passed, boys horsing around, knocking books out of each other's arms, girls laughing and talking. No one nodded "hello" to Mary Jane. No one seemed to notice that she was there.

"They passed me by as if I were a tree," she told herself bitterly. The old feeling that everybody was against her was coming back, real strong now.

"*Je déteste mes ennemis,*" she said out loud. And, having said it, she was about to get up and head for home when she saw Sally crossing the street. Funny little Sally with her red cheeks and her baby clothes and her grown-up way of arguing with teachers. She didn't hate Sally, even though she hated practically everyone else.

Before Sally was within shouting distance Mary Jane could tell from her face that Dr. Green had said "No." "Furry would make too much work for the nurses," she reported, "and they don't have hardly enough anyhow. Nurses, I mean."

Mary Jane nodded glumly as Sally slumped down next to her on the wall. She knew about not enough nurses from Lou Ellen. She really hadn't expected the hospital to take Furry.

"He suggested I call the Humane Society," Sally continued. "You know, where people take sick dogs and lost ones. I mean, one's they've found that don't belong to them. That man at the Humane Society wasn't very nice. He said we should let Furry go or else" — Sally choked, hardly able to finish — "if his foot was hurt real bad, he'd put him to sleep."

Put him to sleep — kill Furry! Mary Jane picked up the cage.

"Where are you going?" Sally asked.

"Home. I mean, I'm going to Grampa's. Really, truly going this time, no matter what anybody says."

Sally's red cheeks paled. "But what about me?"

"You?" Mary Jane paused, surprised. After all, it wasn't Sally the Mothers' League objected to. If Furry had been her squirrel, why then Furry could have stayed in school. Anybody with any brains ought to be able to figure that out.

"I'll miss you." Sally swung her leg, kicking the wall with the heel of her shoe. "I mean, I won't have anybody to be friends with."

"You?" Mary Jane repeated. "But you have everybody in the whole school. You're not like me. I mean, you're — white." There, she'd said it. Now maybe Sally would understand.

"Red," Sally gloomily corrected her. "You don't know how lucky you are, not blushing all the time and being tall. Ever since I was born practically, I've been the smallest kid in the class. The mothers say, 'How cute,' and 'Doesn't she look like a little doll?' But the kids say, 'That baby,' and don't pay attention to me at all."

Mary Jane sank down on the stone wall again. It had never occurred to her that Sally had any problems.

"Clothes — " Sally kept right on complaining.

"You look fine in those new jumpers and straight skirts, but me, I can't buy a single one. I have to go to the children's department to get fitted in these stupid things." She pointed in disgust to the checked gingham dress she was wearing. "Even shoes. Loafers fall right off my feet and they don't make flats small enough for me."

The round blue eyes filled with tears. "I thought it would be better when I got to high school. Thought I'd grow or that people wouldn't care about my size. My sister, when she was here, was president of her class and star in the senior play and everything. Only it's not a bit better. The girls are all in crowds, talking about boys and never anything I want to talk about. Once I said I liked white mice and everybody at lunch laughed. They think I'm funny — funny peculiar!"

"But at lunch," Mary Jane interrupted, "people eat with you. You're not always alone like — "

"Who do I sit with?" Sally sounded angry. "The girls that eat with me, they're the ones nobody else wants. Like Marie who stutters so, can't anybody understand her. I know that's mean, because she can't help stuttering any more than I can help blushing and being short. But still, gee!"

Sally sat with her chin in her hand, staring off into space. Mary Jane tried to think of words to comfort her. "Your father — he's a doctor — couldn't he give you anything? To make you grow?"

"Like in *Alice in Wonderland?* EAT ME and then I open out like a telescope?" Sally couldn't help giggling at the thought. "He says I'll grow. Just to be patient and I'll grow someday."

"That's the way Mamma talks too," Mary Jane sympathized. " 'Just be patient and things'll work out all right.' Only they don't. Do you ever get to feeling sometimes as if everybody's against you?"

"Even my parents." Sally nodded. "I guess it's not their fault, but when I was little — I mean younger — I used to think I was adopted. They're tall and Helen, my sister's tall, but I'm such a shrimp."

Sally sighed. Mary Jane sighed. Furry began to scold. He stretched his paws through the bars of the cage, tugging at Mary Jane's blazer. He was hungry.

"We forgot his food!" Both girls jumped and

ran up the steps and down the long winding
hall that led to the Science room.

The janitor was pushing his big mop along
the corridor floor. "Better hurry," he warned.
"I'm late today on account of the basketball
game and a meeting in the faculty room. But
I'll be locking up soon."

With Furry's cage swinging between them,
they hurried on. Mr. Stiller had gone, but the
birdseed and acorns and crackers and nuts were
still on the closet shelf.

"Can't carry it all," Mary Jane pointed out.
"Let's put some in our schoolbags, enough for
him to eat until — until I get to Grampa's."

"Do you really want to go?" Sally asked as
they set out along the corridor again.

"Not really, I guess." Mary Jane thought
about it. "I'll miss Mamma and Daddy and you.
And I hate for Darlene and that old Mothers'
League to think they chased me away. But what
else can I do with Furry?"

They dawdled in the hall, studying over the
problem. In that whole big building there
wasn't a soul in sight, not even the janitor.
There wasn't a sound to be heard except their
own footsteps and an occasional chirrup from
Furry.

"Creepy, isn't it?" Sally said.

"I kind of like it," Mary Jane answered. "Did you ever pretend you were an explorer, in a jungle maybe, where no human being had ever been before?"

"Or in a cave," Sally suggested. "Exploring a cave and digging up bones from dinosaurs."

"Or the North Pole. Except somebody found that already. Say, let's explore."

"Where?"

"Here. Plenty of places I've never been, right in this school." Mary Jane knew that she shouldn't be suggesting it. The janitor had said "hurry" and she ought to be home breaking open her piggy bank and sneaking off to the bus station. But gosh, it had been so long — months now — since she'd had a friend to talk to. She really wasn't in any rush to run away.

"Where would you like to go?" Sally asked. "I know where things are, sort of, on account of my sister going here."

Sally's statement reminded Mary Jane of the first day of school and the girl who had helped her find her home room. Had that been Sally? Sometime she would ask her, but not now.

Not now, because they were tiptoeing into the Chemistry lab and peeking at the statues of wreathed old Romans in Latin and tramping down the aisle of the big auditorium. They climbed from the orchestra pit to put Furry's cage on Mrs. Davis' special chair. Sitting back on his haunches with his paws pressed against his chest, he chattered away as if he were talking to a student assembly.

They laughed and he chattered and they laughed some more until the big room sent back echoes and they were afraid that the janitor would hear them.

"Come see the rooms backstage," Sally said. "They're real cozy."

She led the way, stepping over coiled ropes, walking around stacked-up scenery, until she found a little door with a big gold star painted on it.

"This is the one Helen had when she was in the senior play. Hope it isn't locked."

The door opened when she rattled the knob, and Mary Jane sat down in one of the room's two straight chairs, with Sally in the other.

"Real cozy," Mary Jane agreed as she looked around. There was a table with a mirror above it, a clothes closet, and a little high window through which she could see the sky. "It would make a dandy clubroom."

Sally jumped and Mary Jane jumped as they both had the exact same thought at the exact same moment. The little dressing room would make a dandy place to keep Furry.

"Nobody ever comes here except when they put on plays, and that won't happen now until Christmas," Sally said.

"The janitor," Mary Jane objected. But when they looked at the dust on the mirror and the dust on the table they felt pretty sure that the janitor didn't come either, except at play times.

"Mrs. Davis," Mary Jane objected again. "I mean suppose we get caught. We'd be in awful trouble."

"Won't get caught." Sally was sure. "Couldn't anybody hear Furry from this room, no matter how loud he squeals. And we can come before school and afterward, to feed him."

Mary Jane stopped objecting. Probably it wasn't the best home in the world for Furry, but it was better than running away when she didn't feel like leaving. And they'd have plenty of time to find some other place before rehearsals for the Christmas play started.

She put Furry's cage on the table, facing the mirror, so that he could think that there was another squirrel in the room keeping him company. She was cramming handfuls of food into the cage when Sally looked at her watch.

"We'd better hurry," she groaned. "If we don't scramble out of here fast, we'll spend the night."

They raced across the stage, through the orchestra pit, and up the auditorium aisle. As they reached the front corridor they could see the janitor's overalled back heading for the door.

"Wait for us," Sally yelled.

He stood in the vestibule, swinging a circle of keys. "It's the squirrel girls, isn't it?" he joked. "If you'd been one minute later, you'd have lived on acorns tonight."

At the corner of South Street they stopped to catch their breaths.

"What time in the morning?"

"Eight? Five after?"

"Five after — in the dressing room," Mary Jane shouted as she ran on down the street.

Outlaws

16

I<small>T WASN'T STORYING</small>, really, when Mary Jane told Mamma that she had to be at school early to take care of Furry. She didn't happen to mention that Furry lived in the star dressing room now instead of on the window sill in Science. After all, you didn't have to tell a mother everything, did you?

As for Fred, when she phoned to say, "Don't come by for me in the morning. I'm leaving early for school," he didn't even think to ask why. These days Fred didn't think about anything but the junior varsity.

Mary Jane tore out of the house in the morning, hoping that Mamma wouldn't notice her bulging schoolbag. Half walking, half running, she arrived at school just when Sally did. They made their way through side doors and back corridors, their hearts beating faster as they approached the little room behind the stage. All kinds of things might have happened to Furry while they were at home.

All kinds of things might have happened — but they didn't. Furry was safe and sound and so excited to see them that he almost toppled his cage. While Mary Jane fetched fresh water from the lavatory in a jar she had hidden in her schoolbag Sally let him out to exercise. He made great leaps from the table to the chairs to the floor, scampering around and scolding because he'd been left alone. What with stroking his head and admiring the way he swished his feathery tail, they hardly had time to clean up before the warning bell rang.

Mary Jane was fastening Furry's cage door when Sally laid a brown paper bag on the table. "Lunch," she explained. "I thought, instead of wasting time in the cafeteria, we could eat down here. I mean, the school says we can't go home for lunch, but there's no rule says we have to eat in the cafeteria. At least not that I've ever heard of."

Mary Jane had never heard of any rule about eating in the cafeteria either. As soon as Math was over, she headed for the star dressing room. Sally had brought peanut-butter sandwiches

and cookies with chocolate icing and the kind
of oranges that are easy to peel. Eating together
with the sun streaming in the little window and
making a square of light on the wall, eating
together with Furry on the table holding an
orange section in his paws, it was as if they
were at a picnic.

"Fabulous," Mary Jane beamed as she popped
a chocolate cookie into her mouth.

"Tremendous," Sally agreed as she took a bite
of orange. "I'm sorry about no milk, though. I
couldn't find our thermos. I figured if we ate
fruit we wouldn't get too terribly thirsty."

"'S fine," Mary Jane mumbled, her mouth
full. "I'll bring milk tomorrow. Only — what did
you tell your mother? I mean, didn't she think
it was funny, the sandwiches and all? I had a
hard enough time taking a jar and some rags
without Mamma seeing."

"Told her I was sick of eating the cafeteria
food, which I am." Sally grinned. "Told her I
wanted to save my allowance for Christmas,
which I do. She said just fine so long as I fixed
the sandwiches myself."

"That's what I'll say too." Mary Jane looked
relieved. "Sure is hard to think of what to tell
them. All last night I was afraid I'd forget and

give us away. It's sort of like we were outlaws, Jesse James or somebody, hiding out from the sheriff."

"Not bad outlaws like Jesse James. Good ones like Robin Hood and Maid Marian. Hiding out from the Mothers' League." Sally giggled.

All during lab period in Science, they whispered, making plans for their secret hiding place. The class was planting beans, planting some deep and others on the surface of flowerpots, watering some well and others not at all, to see which ones would grow best. Mary Jane was pretty sure she knew how the experiment would turn out, and Sally, who had read ahead in the book, was positive that she knew. But they planted the beans the way Mr. Stiller told them to and were glad that in lab period at least they had a chance to talk.

"Hello, you two." Mr. Stiller smiled when he came over to their table to look at their experiment. "How's the squirrel?"

Mary Jane half closed her eyes as she murmured, "Okay," but Sally beamed at him. "Just fine," she reported. "We found him a real good home."

Mary Jane held her breath, afraid that he'd ask more questions and then what would they say? Sally didn't seem the least bit worried. She looked up at him with her round blue eyes and her little girl's face, as innocent as could be. She really enjoyed being an outlaw.

Truth to tell, Mary Jane liked being an outlaw too — for a while. As day followed day and she spent most of her spare time in the room behind the stage, she got used to telling her parents and people like Fred and Mr. Stiller things that were true in a way, only not the whole truth. If her conscience bothered her some as she got into bed at night, she forgot about it in the morning when her alarm clock buzzed and she had to rush in order to meet Sally before home-room period.

Furry was just about the best pet she'd ever had, more cuddly than Curly and lots smarter than Sophie or her long-legged calf. And Sally — well, she was turning out to be a real friend, every bit as good as Gwen or Peggy or Laura had ever been. Of course she was bossy some-times, but she certainly had bright ideas. With the money saved from her allowance, now that she wasn't eating in the cafeteria, she kept buy-ing things for their secret hiding place. Practical things like a wastebasket to keep trash in and paper bags to carry it away, and a bigger elec-

tric light bulb for the light over the table. Mary
Jane spent some of her allowance too, treating
to glasses and a bottle opener and a carton of
cherry soda for thirsty afternoons.

The soda was warm and it fizzed over sometimes when they opened a new bottle, but it
tasted sweet and good. With the door tightly
closed and Furry jumping from the table to the
floor and then climbing up into their laps, it
tasted just fine.

"It's like this is our home, yours and Furry's
and mine," Sally thought. "I mean, everybody's
against the three of us being together. Your
mother, I don't think she really wants me to
come to your house, and mine — "

"My mother does too want you to come,"
Mary Jane interrupted. "It's only that she thinks
yours won't like it. So she says, 'Take it easy —
wait — don't rush things.' "

"Exactly," Sally agreed. "Mother thinks it's
okay that we're friends in school. The very first
day she told me I should act polite to you. She
thought those crowds outside were awful. But
when it comes to bringing you home — that's
different. Then she gets to thinking about what
the neighbors will say."

"Can't change people's feelings all in one

day." Mary Jane mimicked her father's deep voice.

Sally nodded, relieved that Mary Jane understood. "They're actually afraid, my parents are, that people won't ask me to their parties if they know I'm your friend. As if they did anyway — ask me, I mean — and as if I'd want to go to their stupid old parties."

"Your father — " Mary Jane was remembering what her parents had said. "Would sick people really not go to him if — if I came to see you?"

"How'd you know that?"

"Mamma said so."

"Well" — Sally thought it over — "they can't exactly be sure. Personally, I don't believe it, but that's what they say."

"Grownups!" Mary Jane sighed over them for the millionth time while Sally poured more cherry soda and picked up the nutshells Furry was throwing to the floor.

Sipping their soda, they talked about heaps of things. About the girls in their class and how some might turn out to be nice if you could only get to know them. About books they'd read and how they both liked biographies, only not the kind with long descriptions. About what they were going to be when they grew up. Serious things like Mary Jane being a biologist and Sally a doctor, and fun things too, like living on a farm together and having a million or so animal pets.

"Horses and cows and squirrels and pigs and chickens and chipmunks," Mary Jane proposed.

"And a giraffe," Sally insisted. Once the Greens had taken a trip to Washington, where there was a zoo, and she had fallen in love with a long-legged, long-necked baby giraffe.

Mary Jane argued, explaining that giraffes needed a much warmer climate, like Florida or Mexico maybe, but Sally kept saying, "I want a giraffe," until they both started giggling.

Sitting in the little star dressing room, they talked about many things. About boys and clothes and rock 'n roll music, which neither of them liked, and folk songs, which both of them did. One afternoon they even talked about the color of people's skins.

Sally brought that up, blushing crimson all the way to the top button of her blouse. "You're tan, sort of, and Fred, he's brown like, well" — she paused, trying to think of words to describe Fred's color — "like horse chestnuts when they're ripe. And your mother, she's certainly not black. Until I got to know you, though, I always thought — "

Mary Jane listened, not the least bit uncomfortable, wondering what Sally was going to say.

"I always thought that all Negroes looked alike and were different somehow from whites. But now I know — I mean, they're just people like anybody else."

Sally was so flustered that Mary Jane took over the conversation, telling about Red Anne and her Indian father and how there must have been a white great-great-grandpa too, a long time ago. They studied their hands, side by side on the table. Mary Jane's long thin fingers were the color of cinnamon toast; Sally's pudgy hand was close to strawberry-ice-cream color.

She balled it into a fist, trying to hide her well-bitten nails. "Your hand's prettier," she decided.

"Is not," Mary Jane contradicted her. "They're just the same. I mean, yours is pink and mine is brown, but what's the diff?"

"Chr-r-r." Furry broke into the conversation reminding them that today they were going to take off his splints. When the bandage was removed his leg looked fine. He limped only a tiny bit as he climbed to the shelf in the closet for a pawful of crackers. And he didn't seem to be limping at all when he jumped to the table, knocking their soda bottle to the floor.

They went right on talking as they mopped up the soda. About Grampa's farm and a summer camp Sally used to go to and how nice Mr. Stiller was. About mid-terms and marks and taking Latin next year. They talked about everything in the whole world except the Christmas play.

Keeping the secret

17

IT WAS FUN being an outlaw and having a secret hiding place — for a while. Mary Jane whistled when she did her homework and stopped slamming doors and acting cross. Mamma was so pleased to see her cheerful that she bought her a new dress for a surprise. That very same weekend Daddy took her to a drive-in movie and Gwen slept over and walked to Sunday school with her the next day.

Nice things kept happening in school too. Miss Rousseau always asked about Furry and talked about pets she'd had when she was young. She even lent Mary Jane a book about a tame crow who could talk. Mr. Stiller was the nicest of all. One day in Science, when she was telling about Grampa's weed garden, he interrupted her.

"All these times you've spoken of your grand-

father, it never occurred to me before. Is he
the Dr. Charles Douglas, the biologist?"

Mary Jane didn't know how to answer.
Grampa wasn't a doctor, not like Sally's father,
who took care of sick people. But there was a
paper in his desk with Latin writing on it that
Mamma said made him sort of a doctor too.

"I — I — I'm not sure," she stammered. "He's
Charles Douglas and he taught biology at the
state agricultural college, but — "

"Of course he is." Mr. Stiller looked as pleased
as if someone had given him a present. "I
should have guessed. Boys and girls" — he stood
up to emphasize his words — "Mary Jane's
grandfather, Dr. Douglas, has probably done
more for the farmers in this state than any man
alive."

Mary Jane sat tall and proud as he told how
Grampa discovered new crops and taught conservation, told the class things even she didn't
know about Grampa. Darlene slumped in her
seat, doodling on her notebook cover to show
that she wasn't listening, but Mary Jane didn't
care. Almost all of the other boys and girls
seemed real interested.

As she was leaving the room Mr. Stiller called
her over. "I heard him lecture once when I was

a student. He's a grand old man." He wanted
to know if Grampa ever came to High Ridge
for a visit and if she thought he'd come to
Wilson to talk to the Science classes.

Grampa come to Wilson High! Mary Jane's
cheeks burned, and Sally, waiting for her at the
door, blushed in sympathy. At any other time
nothing could have pleased Mary Jane more.
But now, with Mamma and Daddy thinking
Furry lived in the Science room and not knowing about the secret hiding place, with Grampa
sure to find out the truth if he came to school,
what could she say?

She stammered again, promising to write
Grampa and invite him, and all the while knowing that she didn't dare. By the time she
reached the star dressing room she was chewing
on her fingernails just as Sally was and thinking that she didn't always enjoy an outlaw's life.

"It's like eating chocolate ice cream, sort of,"
Sally thought. "The first portion tastes great.
The second's fine. But when you get around to
the third and fourth dish, well, you begin to
start to lose your appetite."

Mary Jane was beginning to lose her appetite
for being an outlaw. She was growing tired of

keeping secrets and not being able to tell people the truth when they were nice.

Fred was hurt because she never came to a single basketball game after that first one, even when she promised. After he noticed that she wasn't eating in the cafeteria, he really scolded.

"How are people going to get to know you if you don't take part in anything and they never see you around? At the beginning you sounded right smart, talking about being a foreign ambassador. But now you might as well not even be in school for all a person sees you."

It was the longest speech Fred had ever made when he wasn't explaining basketball's fine points. Mary Jane couldn't say a word back in her own defense. Even though it was fun in the secret hiding place, she did sometimes think about eating in the cafeteria and how it would be if the other girls saw that she'd made a friend. She did sometimes think, too, that maybe Sally wouldn't want to eat with her right out in front of everybody in the lunchroom.

Furry purred happily in the star dressing room as Sally fed him the remains of her sandwich. Mary Jane put her feet on the table and chewed her nails. "I wish — well — that we didn't have to keep everything so secret all the time."

"Robin Hood" — Sally tried to cheer her up — "he did good deeds, robbing the rich and helping the poor, but he had to hide and keep secrets. Besides, what else can we do?"

What else can we do? That was really what was bothering both of the girls. Every day Furry grew a little bigger and a little stronger. Now that his leg was healed he was entirely too frisky for the parakeet cage. When they locked him up in it, he squawked and squealed. Last weekend, even though they had piled up mountains of food within his reach, he had knocked the cage over and scared himself half to death. Every day Furry was growing bigger — and every day the dates for rehearsals for the Christmas play were drawing nearer.

"Maybe" — Sally was thinking out loud — "we should let him go. Not out in the street where there are cats, but in some nice place, like that grove of oak trees in Calhoun Park. You know, where I got the acorns. We could see him afternoons. He's so tame that I'm sure he'd remember us."

Furry scolded as if he understood what Sally was saying. "You hush," Mary Jane crossly told him. For the first time in weeks her face felt stiff. She busied herself with the cracker boxes on the table so that Sally wouldn't notice. "You could go to the park," she answered without looking up, "but I couldn't."

"You mean your mother won't let you?" Sally was puzzled. "That's silly. Even mine's been letting me play there since I was a baby."

"I mean" — Mary Jane pretended to laugh — "that the park is segregated. There's a sign says 'For Whites Only.' You and Furry would be allowed, but not me."

"Oh, Mary Jane!" Sally was horror-stricken. She jumped up to put her arm around her friend. "I didn't know. Honest I didn't. I never noticed that sign, not once in my life. Can't we — well, just take it down?"

This time Mary Jane really laughed. She couldn't feel hurt when she listened to Sally. Spunky little Sally, who was all ready to go to Calhoun Park and chop down the sign. "But it wouldn't do any good," she pointed out. "Policemen or somebody would chase me. If only — "

She jumped up with a start as she glanced at her watch. If only it wasn't twenty-five after four and they didn't have to rush to put Furry in his cage and dash madly for the front door before the janitor locked it. Scurrying about, they gave Furry his supper and his water and an extra pile of acorns for a midnight snack. They could still hear him scolding as they stumbled over the scenery backstage.

"I feel like Cinderella hurrying home from the ball," Sally complained. "I'll lose my shoe and my schoolbag'll turn into a pumpkin — "

"And there's the prince coming to your rescue." Mary Jane half giggled, half groaned as she saw the janitor walking out of the vestibule, away from the front door, with his big ring of keys swinging from his belt.

If the janitor was a prince, he was an awfully huffy one. Before he would unlock the door to let them out, he gave them a long lecture about girls who were late and made extra work for busy people. On the step outside they paused, surprised to find that it was almost dark.

"The days are getting shorter," Sally pointed out.

Mary Jane nodded. Nobody needed to tell her what Sally was thinking. Across the street she could see a store window decorated with pictures of Pilgrims and turkeys and garlands of Indian corn. Other years, Thanksgiving meant that James would be home from college for the weekend, that maybe Grampa would visit. Other years, Thanksgiving meant turkey and mince pie and family and fun.

This year, Thanksgiving meant that Christmas was coming — and, with Christmas, the rehearsals for the school play.

Not really a vandal

18

IT HAPPENED the very next morning. In home room, Miss Rousseau picked up her daily bulletin and started reading it aloud. "Tryouts for the Christmas play today at three in the auditorium."

Mary Jane sat there chewing a fingernail, scarcely listening. Because something much worse had already taken place. Furry was gone. When she and Sally had arrived at the star dressing room at eight, the door was ajar and the parakeet cage on the floor. There was a trail of cracker crumbs around the sets backstage, but Furry wasn't anywhere in sight.

Sally gulped, turning scarlet, then pale. "We rushed so yesterday. I guess I didn't close the door tight. He must have knocked over the cage and then — "

And then where could he have gone? For

anxious moments they called and clucked and cooed. They tried chirruping like a squirrel and shouting like two girls. They clambered around the scenery and they looked behind the drapes and inside the coiled-up rings of rope. They searched the stage and the orchestra pit and turned up every single seat in the auditorium, even in the balcony. But they didn't find Furry.

Mary Jane sat in home room feeling perfectly blank. She was hardly paying attention when Mrs. Davis' voice came over the public address system. "Very serious," the principal said. "Vandalism . . . food strewn all over the cafeteria . . . dishes broken . . . malicious mischief."

Mary Jane straightened up, dropping her hand on her desk. What was Mrs. Davis saying? "If the culprits confess before noon . . . otherwise the police . . . disgrace to the school."

Mary Jane's heart thumped and she couldn't answer when Miss Rousseau called on her in French. All during English she stared out of the window, chewing first on her underlip, then on her nails. By the time the period bell rang she had made up her mind.

Sally was waiting for her in the corridor. Even Sally, spunky little Sally, looked scared. "The

vandal," she moaned. "It must be Furry. We'll
have to — "

"Tell Mrs. Davis," Mary Jane finished for her.

Reaching for each other's hand, they walked
down the stairs to the principal's office. The
door was closed, and Mary Jane rapped on it
with her knuckles once, twice, until they heard
a blurred "Come in."

She dropped Sally's hand as they crossed the
room to stand in front of the principal's desk.
Mrs. Davis looked sternly at them over her
glasses.

"Yes, girls?" she asked.

"We think — that is — " Mary Jane swallowed
hard.

"Not really malicious mischief," Sally started
in a faint little voice. "He doesn't know any
better."

"Sit down," the principal said. "Are you girls
trying to tell me that you know who the vandal
is?"

They perched on the edge of their chairs,
looking just as uncomfortable as they felt. "We
think we know," Mary Jane said, "but — "

"But he's not really a vandal," Sally added.

"And what would you call him when he
breaks cups and glasses and tosses bags of pea-

nuts and potato chips all over the cafeteria?"
Mrs. Davis angrily asked.

The two girls exchanged doleful glances.
After hearing about the peanuts, there was no
longer any doubt in their minds.

"A squirrel," they chorused.

"A squirrel?" Mrs. Davis dropped the pencil
she was holding and stared at them openmouthed.

Mary Jane gulped and choked and stammered, and Sally turned deeper and deeper
shades of red. Slowly they told their story, while
Mrs. Davis studied her pencil and lifted her
eyebrows and listened to every word. If perhaps once or twice the corners of her mouth
turned up a little, Mary Jane and Sally were too
upset to notice.

"All you really know," she summed up when
they were finished, "is that your squirrel is loose
somewhere in the school. He may not even be
in the cafeteria."

"Maybe not now," Mary Jane sighed, "but
he's been there. He's awfully good at finding
food, especially peanuts."

"And throwing things around when he's had
enough," Sally said.

Mrs. Davis looked at her watch. "You've

broken I don't know how many school rules, in addition to several that I never thought of making. But before I consider disciplinary action you'd better find that squirrel. You have just twenty minutes before first lunch."

Broken rules . . . disciplinary action. Two unhappy girls followed Mrs. Davis down the hall. The cafeteria had been tidied, and at a table near the cashier's desk several teachers were eating an early lunch. Mary Jane hung her head even lower as she recognized Mr. Stiller and Miss Rousseau. Now they were going to find out about all the storying she had done.

Mrs. Davis joined the teachers while Mary Jane and Sally stood uncertainly in the center aisle, between the rows of long tables.

"Chrr, chrr-rr," Sally trilled, trying to sound like a squirrel.

"Here, Furry. Here, Furry," Mary Jane called.

Out of the corners of her eyes she could see the teachers watching. Mr. Stiller, Miss Rousseau, the very nicest teachers in the whole school. She blinked, fighting back tears.

"Chrr, chrr . . . Here Furry." Up and down the aisle they walked, calling softly at first and then at the top of their lungs.

At last there was an answer. Furry was sitting

on a curtain rod as close to the high ceiling as he could get. Sitting and scolding, with no intention at all of coming down. Mary Jane begged and Sally pleaded, while Mr. Stiller got up to close the cafeteria door. Furry ran along the top of the curtains, making graceful little leaps from one window to another and waving his feathery tail as if he were showing it off.

"Try this." Miss Rousseau offered Mary Jane a slice of bread.

Waving the bread, Mary Jane called to Furry in her most loving voice. Finally Furry scrambled down, jumping from the window to the floor, while all the people in the room held their breaths. Two flicks of his tail, two bounds, and he was at Mary Jane's feet. When she stooped to pick him up, he jumped to her shoulder. Grabbing the bread from her hand, he started to eat.

"Like an act in the circus." Someone at the teachers' table clapped until Mrs. Davis looked up with a frown.

"The first lunch will be in here in a minute," she said. "Mind you hold him tight, Mary Jane, while you bring him to my office. I don't want him loose in that crowd."

"Maybe I can help." Mr. Stiller left his table to follow Mrs. Davis and the girls.

"I too." Miss Rousseau joined them as the buzz of the lunch bell echoed through the room.

It was a strange procession, Mrs. Davis in the lead, followed by Sally and Mary Jane and Furry, with Mr. Stiller and Miss Rousseau bringing up the rear. The boys and girls swarming out of their classrooms paused to stare.

Mary Jane buried her face in the squirrel's fur. *"Je m'en moque,"* she said to herself as she followed the principal. But that was silly. Of course she cared. She didn't want to lose Furry or be suspended from school or anything.

Sally looked up sympathetically, her face scarlet and her blue eyes round, as they reached the door of the principal's office. They filed in, one, two, three, four, five silent people and a frisky gray squirrel who was cheerfully waving a battered slice of bread.

Before Mrs. Davis had a chance to say anything, Mr. Stiller cleared his throat. "May we sit in on this, Miss Rousseau and I?" he asked. "We — I — feel sort of responsible. I knew these girls had a problem, but I'm sorry to say I didn't take the time to find out how they'd solved it."

"I feel responsible too," Miss Rousseau added

in her low funny-accented voice. "Mary Jane's in my home room. It was hard for her at first and lonely, but lately — "

"I know," Mrs. Davis interrupted, looking so stern that Mary Jane wondered if she really did know.

"Nevertheless," Mrs. Davis continued, "people can't solve their problems at the expense of the school. Because a student is having difficulties doesn't mean he can do whatever he likes."

Sally fixed her eyes on the corner of the rug, and Mr. Stiller looked gloomy. It was just then that Furry decided to jump from Mary Jane's lap to Mrs. Davis' desk. And to sit on his haunches, impudently offering the principal a bite of his gnawed bread.

Mary Jane sat glued to her chair, not daring to move. Now Mrs. Davis would really be mad. Why did Furry have to pick the worst possible moment to misbehave?

The principal tried hard to frown at Furry, but her lips twitched and at last she gave way to laughter. "He is irresistible, isn't he? I can see why you girls hated to give him up." She stroked Furry's head while he waved his bushy tail over the papers on her desk, and Mary Jane and Sally held their breaths.

"I ought to give you at the very least a month's detention," the principal continued. "but since this is your first violation of school rules, I'll let you off with a warning — this time. Only you understand, of course, you can't keep your squirrel in school any longer."

Cradling Furry in her arms, Mary Jane mumbled her thanks. Mrs. Davis could have suspended her or kept her after school for a month or written a letter home to Mamma. Mrs. Davis could have done any of these things, but she didn't. Mary Jane was still scared of her, the way everybody in seventh grade was, but she didn't feel half bad. Because Mrs. Davis certainly wasn't against her.

I can't go

19

As soon as school was over, they had a conference in the Science room, Mary Jane and Sally, Mr. Stiller and Miss Rousseau. Mr. Stiller sat on one of the high tables, swinging his legs and making suggestions about a home for Furry. The Humane Society, the park, places that Mary Jane and Sally had thought of long ago and turned down.

"I'd offer to keep him myself, but I have only a small place, just a room," he said. "And I'm afraid that my landlady wouldn't take to him at all. Fact is, he's close to full grown now, really too big to be caged."

"But he's so tame," Miss Rousseau pointed out. "I'm afraid he wouldn't survive very long on the streets. It's not only cats, but cars."

Mary Jane sighed. Sally sighed. Miss Rousseau twisted a lock of her hair, the way Mamma did when she was thinking.

"I've got it!" Mr. Stiller slid off the table to stand by the window sill next to Furry's cage. "He's too big to live indoors, too tame for city streets. But how about the country? How about your grandfather's farm?"

"Fabulous!" Mary Jane beamed her approval of the idea. "We couldn't see him terribly often, but he'd be safe there. And I know just where he could live." She was telling about the hickory tree near the barn, when she caught sight of Sally's face.

"Be nice for you and your grampa," Sally said in a polite little voice. "And for Furry, of course."

"But — but — Grampa'd love to have you visit too," Mary Jane assured her. "He's not — well, funny like most grownups are. And it would give you a chance to see Curly and Sophie and the chickens and all."

Sally turned redder than Mary Jane had ever seen her. "My mother and father — " She broke off, choking and swallowing as if something were stuck in her throat.

Her mother and father. Sally was trying to say that her mother and father wouldn't let her visit Grampa's farm. Not visit Grampa, who was practically the most wonderful person in the world. Mary Jane turned away to look out of the window with blurred eyes. She hated them, hated Dr. and Mrs. Green and even, for a moment, she hated Sally.

The two girls sat there like statues, not moving, not saying a word. It was as if they were strangers instead of best friends.

"Maybe I can help." Mr. Stiller broke the silence. "Ever since I was in college I've wanted to meet Dr. Douglas. If I drove you out there on Saturday — you two girls and the squirrel — "

"And me," Miss Rousseau interrupted.

"If I wrote a note to your father" — he nodded at Sally — "I think he'd permit you to come. For a girl who's interested in science, it could be a very educational trip."

Sally's face brightened. "Would you do that? I mean, tell him it's sort of like a field trip, like to a museum or something? I really think that'll work."

Mary Jane felt mixed up and a little bit angry. After all, Grampa wasn't a museum. He was a live man, "a grand old man" Mr. Stiller had called him. A person ought to be glad to have his child pay him a visit. But she couldn't keep

on being angry, because Sally and Mr. Stiller
and Miss Rousseau were so pleased with their
solution to the problem. Sally couldn't help it
about her parents. It was the way they had been
brought up, that's all.

She smiled along with everyone else and said
she'd phone Grampa that very night to ask if
they could come, but it would be all right with
him, she was sure. And Mr. Stiller said he'd
brave his landlady and keep Furry in his room
until their Saturday trip.

After everyone had helped to carry Furry and
his cracker boxes and birdseed down to Mr.
Stiller's car and Sally had turned at her corner
to head for home, Mary Jane crossed the street.
She walked in and out of the five-and-ten and
stopped to buy some pencils at the stationery
store and to study the sweaters in the window
of a dress shop. She even considered going to
the library to take out a book. Because the
longer she put off going home, the longer it
would be before she would have to tell Mamma
about Furry's life in Wilson High.

Mamma scolded and so did Daddy. For one
terrible moment it seemed as if they might for-
bid the Saturday expedition. But then they said
that since it had all been arranged with Mr.

Stiller and Miss Rousseau she could go ahead and telephone Grampa.

Truth to tell, they weren't half bad, considering all the storying she had done. That was the confusing thing about grownups. Sometimes they didn't seem to understand a thing and other times they knew lots more than you expected them to.

Over the phone Grampa didn't ask a single question. Just said he'd look forward to meeting Sally and the teachers and any squirrel that was a friend of Mary Jane's. He sounded so good, joking the way he always did, that Mary Jane thought of phoning Sally to tell her about it. She even looked up Sally's number in the telephone book before she decided that it was best not to call. She phoned Fred instead, to say she'd walk to school with him in the morning and watch the next junior varsity game.

There wasn't time to speak to Sally before home-room period. All morning long Mary Jane wondered what her parents had said and what she was going to do about lunch, now that they could no longer eat in their secret hideaway. As Math class drew to a close she felt just the least little bit uncertain. Should she fortify herself with a book in case — well, just in case she was eating alone?

When the bell rang and everybody tore out of class to be first in the lunch line, Mary Jane dawdled. She fiddled around with her books and her locker until she was trailing far behind the crowd. She walked toward the cafeteria with her head high and her nose up in the air. She was so busy looking unconcerned that she walked right past Sally, who was waiting at the door.

"Hey, wake up. You look as if you're walking in your sleep," Sally teased. "Where you been so late?"

Mary Jane looked down at her friend with a sheepish smile. "What're you doing so early?" she teased back as they took their places in line.

Sandwiches, jello, milk, napkins, spoons. With loaded trays they trudged along the cafeteria aisle. Mary Jane caught her breath as she saw people lift their heads and nudge their neighbors. Sally kept on talking as if nothing special were happening. She walked down the aisle until she spotted a table where there were a few empty seats.

"Okay?" she asked.

"Okay." Mary Jane nodded.

There was silence at the table as they put down their trays, but nobody actually got up and walked away. By the time they started on their sandwiches people were talking noisily again. Just as if this wasn't the very first time that Mary Jane had eaten in the Wilson cafeteria with her friend.

"My father" — Sally had saved the good news until they sat down — "he says it's all right for Saturday. He gave me a note to Mr. Stiller saying I could go. If it's all right with your grampa, that is."

"Grampa says fine." Mary Jane sipped her milk, trying not to show her relief. "Did you catch it? When you got home, I mean."

"Plenty." Sally grinned ruefully. "They bawled me out all through dinner. *Helen* never got into any trouble at school. *She* never had to go to the principal's office."

"Not Lou Ellen either that I ever heard of," Mary Jane sighed.

"If it hadn't been for Mr. Stiller's letter, don't know what they'd have done. But after they were all finished scolding, Mother just said no television for a week."

"Same with mine. And that's not bad really. Say, you want to go to the basketball game this afternoon? Fred says it's going to be real good."

Sally wanted to go, and after Science they put their books in their lockers and walked downstairs to the gym. Going with Sally wasn't quite the same as going with Furry. A few people stared when they came in. A few people stopped talking as they found seats on one of the long benches that lined the court. But after the game started, everybody was too busy watching the players to pay attention to Sally and Mary Jane.

Fred dribbled the ball down the court, making basket after basket, while Mary Jane yelled until she was hoarse. When the cheerleaders leaped into the air, chanting "Rah, rah, Jackson! Rah, rah, team!" she felt — well, really part of the school.

She even hummed a little, trying out "Wilson Our Alma Mater" as she walked along the corridor to meet Sally for lunch the next day. She had almost gotten the tune when she saw Sally. Saw her puffy eyes and swollen nose and her droopy, slumping shoulders.

"I can't go to the farm tomorrow." Sally's lower lip quivered as she announced the news.

"Whyever not?"

"Because I — because — well, they told me

not to tell you. They told me to say I had to go someplace with them."

Mary Jane's face froze. No need to ask who "they" were. Sally's parents weren't going to let her go to Grampa's. She started to walk away.

Sally put her hand on her arm. "It's not even exactly their fault. I mean, the phone calls were something fierce. 'Did you know your daughter eats lunch with the Negro girl?' 'Did you know they went to the basketball game together?' 'I just thought you ought to know — '" Sally angrily mimicked ladies' voices.

Mary Jane's face was cold and there were goose-pimples all along her arms, but she opened her eyes wide and tried for a smile. This was Sally, her friend, she reminded herself. It wasn't her fault what other people did.

"Mother was fine at first," Sally continued. "She just said, 'Thank you for calling,' and didn't seem to care. Until they started phoning Daddy at his office. That's when she got upset."

Mary Jane nodded politely, as if Sally were speaking of something that was happening in China or Timbuktu and not to her.

"She talked it over with my father, and then they both talked to me. For hours. Said this is still a Southern city and there are some things we can't do, no matter how we feel about them. Maybe later on, when feelings die down, but not now. Said they were sorry, but, well, I can't go to the farm."

"How about, I mean — in school?" Mary Jane couldn't finish the question.

Sally tossed her head. "I said they couldn't make us not be friends. I said I was going to eat with you in school every single day and there wasn't anything they could do to stop me. No matter how many people telephoned. They argued quite a bit, but finally they said it would be okay in school, only not outside."

Mary Jane would have whistled her relief if Sally hadn't looked so unhappy. After all, it was Sally who was going to miss the trip with the two teachers, Sally who wouldn't see Furry any more or get to meet Grampa.

"I'll remember every single thing that happens and tell you about it on Monday." She tried to comfort her.

Two big tears rolled down Sally's cheeks and she angrily wiped them away. "You'd think that when people were grown-up they'd have more sense," she grumbled.

Good-by, Furry

20

On Saturday, Mr. Stiller parked in the Douglases' driveway at eight-thirty sharp, with Miss Rousseau on the front seat beside him and Furry on the floor in the back. They waited to say "Hello" to Mamma and Daddy and to find out the best road to the farm. And then they were off.

It was one of those almost-winter days when you can see your breath puff out in front of you early in the morning. Then later, with the sun shining and no clouds at all in the sky, it gets warm and you unbutton your jacket and take the scarf off your head. Especially if your mother isn't around to make a fuss about catching cold.

As soon as they were out on the highway, Mary Jane rolled down the window. Starlings and sparrows were the only birds in High Ridge this time of year, but all along the road there

were chickadees and juncos and families of redbirds darting in and out of thornbush thickets
and eating holly berries. Miss Rousseau turned
in her seat to talk about the birds while Furry
ran back and forth in his cage as if he knew he
was going to a nice place where there would be
grass and trees.

After a while, with the sun shining in through
the car windows and the wind carrying hay
smells and dried sweet clover, Mary Jane forgot
that she was riding with two teachers from her
school. Miss Rousseau sang songs in French and
Mr. Stiller joined in on the choruses in a voice
as loud and flat as Grampa's. After a while Mary
Jane chimed in too. She and Mr. Stiller sang
country songs like

"The next to come in and was a little flea
To dance a jig with the bumblebee"

while Miss Rousseau laughed and Furry
scolded, not approving of the noise.

Laughing and singing, it seemed hardly any
time at all before Mr. Stiller turned off the
highway to the country road that led straight
to the farm. Mary Jane lifted up Furry's cage
so that he could look at the trees and distant

hills — and at Grampa, who was waiting for them on the steps of his porch.

Grampa looked the same as he always did, with a pipe in his hand and a flower in the buttonhole of his faded blue shirt. Mary Jane felt grownup-proud as she introduced him to her new friends and listened to Mr. Stiller call him "sir" and Miss Rousseau say "Pleased to meet you, Dr. Douglas." Only it sounded more like "Docteur-r Dooglas" because of the way she rolled her *r*'s.

"Where's — ?" Mary Jane thought Grampa was going to say, "Where's Sally?" Instead he bent down to scratch Furry's head. "Where are you planning to put your squirrel?" he asked.

Before going into the house or even looking for Curly, Mary Jane carried Furry's cage over to the hickory tree next to the barn and opened its door. With a chitter of delight the squirrel bounded from the cage to the tree, climbing up and up and up until he was silhouetted against the sky. From branch to branch he scampered, exploring, running, leaping, with his feathery tail rippling behind him almost as if he were dancing. From branch to branch, from the tree to the barn roof, from the barn to the tree, and then down the trunk to show Mary Jane a hickory nut he had found. His black eyes were bright with excitement, and he jerked his tail back and forth before climbing the tree again.

Mary Jane felt half glad, half sad. "Like a mother, I guess, with her child going out into the world to seek his fortune." She laughed. She didn't say the rest of what she was thinking — if only Sally were here.

"No doubt about it, this is the place for him." Mr. Stiller was pleased. "Better than the star dressing room, eh, Mary Jane?"

Mary Jane nodded, looking sideways at Grampa to see if he'd ask what her teacher meant. But Grampa only rumpled her hair and said, "Come say hi to Curly."

Curly waggled his corkscrew tail and waddled after the visitors as they inspected the barn and the chicken yard and opened the gate to the pasture. Sophie was too busy foraging for food to look up, but the calf walked over to be patted and to lick Mary Jane's hand with her rough black tongue.

"She still remembers me." Mary Jane was delighted.

"Of course she does." Grampa chuckled. "Why, she was saying to me only the other day, 'When's that girl coming to give me a name? Can't have people calling me "Sophie's calf" now that I'm grown.'"

Probably it was silly, but something about the calf's friendly brown eyes made Mary Jane think of round blue ones. "Sally," she announced without hesitation. "We'll name her Sally, after my friend from school."

Tilting her head, she looked up at Grampa, plainly challenging him to ask where Sally was. Still Grampa didn't ask. All he said was, "Miss Calf, I hereby christen you 'Sally,'" and laughed when the calf twitched her tail and answered with a solemn "Mo-o-o."

Even when they sat down to lunch at a table that had been set for five people Grampa didn't mention Sally. Mr. Stiller admired the country-cured ham, and the salad greens reminded Miss Rousseau of salads they had in France. By the time Grampa took a pumpkin pie from the kitchen window they were busily discussing men cooks. That is, the grownups talked about cooking while Mary Jane ate and ate and ate. When she'd finished two pieces of pie and three glasses of Sophie's creamy milk, she wriggled around in her seat, wishing that they'd talk about something else.

"Haven't paid much attention to you, chicka-dee." Grampa reached around to tweak her pony tail. "Haven't even admired that new haircut. From the rear, you call to mind Mr. Lancaster's brown colt."

Before Mary Jane had a chance to tease back, Mr. Stiller asked Grampa about farm horses and whether he favored bluegrass or some other kind of feed. Horses led to mules, and mules led to tractors, and goodness only knows where tractors might have led to if Mary Jane hadn't coughed good and loud. It wasn't very polite, but it was the only way she could think of to break into a conversation that had gone on without her far too long.

When she finally had everyone looking at her, she wasn't sure what she wanted to say. "Sally" — she hesitated — "Sally said to tell you she was sorry she couldn't come."

Grampa took out his pouch and filled his pipe, tamping down the tobacco with his forefinger in that slow careful way he had. "I take it you mean Sally-the-girl and not Sally-the-calf." He was starting to joke, until he saw Mary Jane's face.

She felt a little cross with Grampa. The trouble was that she wanted to tell him about Dr. and Mrs. Green and she didn't want to tell him, both at the same time.

He puffed on his pipe before continuing. "I figured if she didn't come it was because she

had to go someplace with her mother and father," he suggested.

Mary Jane rolled her eyes around, looking at
Mr. Stiller and Miss Rousseau. Their faces were
perfectly straight. She could just say "Yes" to
Grampa and let it go at that. Or she could tell
him the truth.

"Her parents wouldn't let her come." She
blurted it out at last. "Because you're a Negro
and I'm a Negro, they wouldn't let her come."

Grampa walked to the stove to fetch more
coffee for the two teachers. "I figured it could
also be something like that," he observed.

"She wanted to come" — Mary Jane defended
her friend — "the worst way, she wanted to
come, but it was the mean old parents of the
family said 'No.'"

"Can't truly fault them for it without trying
to understand," Grampa said. "They haven't
been raised to all these changes like you and
Sally have. Tell me, how'd you two come to be
friends in the first place?"

Wrinkling her forehead, Mary Jane thought
back to the opening days of school. She told
Grampa about the little girl who had helped
her find her home room and the time Sally had
asked to be her partner in folk dancing.

"Then right at the beginning, without even

knowing you, she was friendly?" Grampa sounded surprised. "How'd that happen, do you suppose?"

"Her mother," Mary Jane reluctantly admitted. "Her mother said she should be polite to me."

"Her mother," Mr. Stiller added, "spoke out for integration of the schools. Stirred up quite a fuss last year. Some people even talked of asking Dr. Green to resign from the hospital board."

"Aha," Grampa said, as if he'd made a big discovery. "That so?" Leaning back in his chair, he studied the bowl of his pipe.

Mary Jane frowned impatiently. Grampa never got mad, not ever, at a single solitary soul. Probably that's what came of being so old. Anyone could see what he was leading up to — that Sally's parents must be pretty nice after all. Well, she was young and she didn't agree with him.

Surprisingly enough, neither did Miss Rousseau. She put down her coffee cup with a bang. "I wouldn't — how do you say it? — fault Mary Jane for getting angry with the Greens. This foolishness about race and color — for educated people, it's just nonsense," she spluttered.

"Foolishness, of course." Mr. Stiller tried to

soothe her. "But you've got to understand that it takes courage for the Greens to speak out even a little in a town like High Ridge."

"Pouf," Miss Rousseau retorted. "If they're so brave, why isn't Sally on the farm with us today?"

Exactly. Mary Jane nodded her agreement. Grampa took his pipe out of his mouth as if he were about to speak, but before he could start, Mr. Stiller pushed back his chair.

Pacing the room, he answered Miss Rousseau. "Because they're not *that* brave, that's why. But maybe they will be next year. If Dr. Green loses his position on the hospital board — "

"Pouf!" Miss Rousseau's eyes flashed her indignation. "Worse things have happened to a man than losing his job."

Mr. Stiller got red in the face and waggled a finger at Miss Rousseau. She kept answering him back and saying "Pouf!" until he was practically yelling. Mary Jane smothered a giggle behind her hand. It was fun listening to them argue as if they were ordinary people and not two teachers from Wilson High. Besides, she was interested to hear what they were saying.

Grampa blew big smoke rings and gave a

slow, secret wink toward Mary Jane. When it looked as if Mr. Stiller was going to hit the table with his fist, he stepped in to make peace.

"You're both right, of course," he said. "No need to pin medals on people because they act like decent human beings some of the time. On the other hand, there certainly is a difference between folks like the Greens and those others who were up at the school on opening day."

"Darlene's mother," Mary Jane interrupted. "And those women from the Mothers' League."

"When I saw this child's picture in the paper, with those people jeering at her — " Grampa put his pipe down. "There's a gun in the attic hasn't been used since the Spanish-American War. I tell you, I came mighty close to oiling it and carrying it up to town."

Mary Jane blinked in surprise. Grampa, who wouldn't even kill a chicken hawk, was talking about shooting a gun! Of course he didn't really mean it, but it was good to know that even he got mad sometimes.

It seemed to make Mr. Stiller and Miss Rousseau feel better too. Or at least they stopped arguing with each other and switched to talk about wars. About the Korean War, when Mr.

Stiller had been a soldier, and World War II, when the Germans had occupied France, and the Spanish-American one that Grampa had fought in.

Wars weren't very interesting to Mary Jane. She soon excused herself to go outside and look for Furry. Standing under the hickory tree, she whistled good and loud on a piece of grass until he came scrabbling down the trunk. She balanced him on her shoulder to show him a chipped old birdbath near the house where he could find water. When he leaped away to climb his tree again, she went into the barn to fetch him some corn.

Miss Rousseau found her in the barn. Grampa and Mr. Stiller were in the little greenhouse off the kitchen. With Mr. Stiller almost as interested in plants as Grampa was, they were sure to be there for a long time. Which meant that Mary Jane and Miss Rousseau — and Curly — could wander through the pasture and down to the brook at the farthest end of Grampa's farm.

The trees in the wood lot were casting shadows across the field as they trudged back. It was time to lead Sophie and Sally-the-calf to the barn. Time to return to High Ridge.

Grampa and Mr. Stiller were standing near

the car, waiting for them. "Say good-by to Furry now," the teacher called. "I promised your mother I'd get you back for supper."

Mary Jane stood under the hickory tree, but this time Furry didn't come when she called. The grownups joined her, whistling and halloing, until at last there was a flash of fur at the barn door. Furry no longer needed anybody to fetch him corn. He was running across the grass, half dragging, half carrying an ear that he'd stolen from the bin.

"At least" — Mary Jane grinned up at Grampa — "I won't have to worry about your remembering to feed him."

"That's not my worry either." Grampa grinned back. "The question is, will he leave enough corn for my chickens?"

After that it was really good-by. Good-by to Grampa and Furry and a wet smack on the cheek from Curly's snout. As Mr. Stiller started up the motor, Grampa poked his head in the back window.

"Tell Sally Furry sends his love and we hope to see her one of these days."

Wanted: An igloo

21

LIFE AT SCHOOL was simpler without Furry. Mary Jane and Sally missed him, of course, but there was Thanksgiving coming and tests this week and another junior varsity game to go to. Mary Jane stopped chewing her fingernails and Sally kept resolving to stop and then forgetting all about her resolution. They met in the corridors between classes and talked in the lavatory and ate lunch together in the cafeteria until most people got used to the idea that they were friends. Some of the girls at their table were even beginning to talk to Mary Jane, although some didn't talk at all.

When school was out in the afternoons the two of them sat on the stone wall at the edge of the lawn, swinging their feet and discussing all sorts of subjects — horses and hairdos and how they wished they could fly in a plane right around the world. Sitting on the wall watching the boys fooling around and the girls walking home together, they felt almost as cozy as they had in their secret hideaway.

Sitting on the wall was fine when the sun was shining. But the week after Thanksgiving it rained every single day except for the day that it snowed. Even the snow wasn't the nice kind that the boys made snowballs with. It was slushy and gray and wet, so that a person didn't feel like going outside and had to wear boots when she did.

Mary Jane and Sally sloshed across the street to wander around in the stores. They looked over everything on the five-and-ten counters and they spent so long at the stationer's pretending that they were going to buy a notebook if they could only find the right kind that the owner of the store began to scowl at them.

"Now where?" Mary Jane asked as they stood in the doorway, wishing that the snow would stop.

"I'm tired," Sally complained. "Let's go someplace where we can sit. Let's go to the drugstore and buy a coke."

Mary Jane made a face. "I don't think — I'm not sure — I don't think they'll sell me one."

"Pouf," Sally said, copying Miss Rousseau.

"Of course they will. They're nice people. I've been there lots of times."

She was so sure of herself and it was so cold and damp in the doorway that Mary Jane gave in. They marched into the drugstore and sat down side by side on the high stools.

"Two cokes," Sally boldly announced.

The woman behind the counter picked up two glasses and turned toward the faucet to fill them. When she noticed Mary Jane, she put them down.

"You, yes." She jerked her head toward Sally. "But not her. If she's thirsty, I'll give her the coke in a paper cup and she can drink it outside."

Sally turned so red that she was almost purple. She wanted to stay and argue with the woman, but when she looked around Mary Jane was gone. She was standing outside under the drugstore awning with her head high and her nose pointed toward the gray sky.

"Darn it." Sally slammed the door behind her as hard as she could. "I'm awful sorry."

"Doesn't matter," Mary Jane informed her, her nose still up in the air. "It's happened before and it'll happen again. Only — well, where'll we go now?"

Shrugging her shoulders, Sally led the way across the street back to school. It was warm in the vestibule and they shook out their scarves and wiped the snowflakes from their faces. Mary Jane sneezed and Sally sighed.

"Wilson" — she thought out loud — "it's like neutral territory, like Switzerland during a war. I mean, even with Darlene and the Mothers' League, it's about the only place we can be friends."

"It's going to feel like Switzerland pretty soon," Mary Jane tried to joke. "What're we going to do if it really snows?"

"We'll build an igloo next to the school steps," Sally joked back. "If the Eskimos can do it, so can we."

Joking was all very well, but when it kept on raining and snowing and sleeting, they got tired of loitering in the school corridors. Students weren't allowed to sit in the classrooms after three, unless they were being kept in, and even the door of the school library was closed. Truth to tell, there wasn't any place for Sally and Mary Jane to go when their feet were tired and they wanted to sit down.

"Maybe" — Mary Jane was doubtful — "we should try out for girls' basketball. I'm not good like Fred, but probably they'd let me try. If we were substitutes even we'd have a chance to talk in the gym."

Sally groaned. "Probably they wouldn't mind your color, but what about my size? Those girls on the basketball team, even the ones in our class, are feet taller than I am. However, if you want to sign up," she added politely, "that's perfectly all right with me."

"Dope." Mary Jane scolded. "I don't especially like playing basketball. I was just trying to find us a home."

For the thousandth time Mary Jane started, "If only we were grown up," and Sally finished, "and could do whatever we wanted."

Sauntering along without thinking of where they were going, they found themselves at the entrance of the auditorium. Through the padded door they could hear noises. People were talking, a piano playing.

"Christmas play," Sally remembered. "They're rehearsing now."

"Maybe we could — "

Sally shook her head. "That Miss Clinton who runs Dramatics, she still thinks we're fighting the Civil War. I honestly don't think she'd give you a part."

"That wasn't my idea," Mary Jane explained. "I thought we could sit way back in the auditorium. If we didn't make noise, wouldn't anybody notice we were there. Or even if they notice, probably they wouldn't care."

"Great idea," Sally approved. She was reaching for the handle of the door when they heard a deep voice behind them.

"Oh no! Not there, after all the trouble you got into the last time." It was Mr. Stiller, pretending to be upset because they were entering the auditorium.

Sally and Mary Jane jumped back guiltily, even though they hadn't been doing anything wrong.

"We were only going in to sit, not go backstage."

". . . to have a place where we can talk."

"Why don't you go —— " The teacher started to ask and then stopped. "You mean to say —— " He tried again, looking uncomfortable.

Both girls answered him at once. "Not my house or hers . . ."

"Not the drugstore . . ."

"Since the rain . . ."

"The school's our only place where we can be together."

Mr. Stiller looked angry, the way he had
when he was arguing with Miss Rousseau. Only
he wasn't angry with Sally or Mary Jane.
"Adults," he growled. "While we're settling all
the problems of the world, we forget about you
kids. We say 'next year' and 'patience.' Only
you two, you can't wait, can you?"

"We can't wait," Sally solemnly agreed.

He scratched his head, thinking. "Come on
up to the Science room. Maybe we can figure
out something."

They followed him up the stairs and along
the corridor to the empty Science room. The
white mice were spinning around on the exercise wheel in their cage and the fish were staring openmouthed through the glass wall of the
aquarium. Mr. Stiller sat between the mice and
the fish and thought.

He kept on thinking until Sally couldn't stay
quiet any longer. "What we need's an igloo."
She giggled.

"There's never enough snow in High Ridge,"
Mary Jane contradicted her. "I'm saving up for
a waterproof tent."

"Maybe" — Sally looked slyly at Mr. Stiller —
"maybe we could come here afternoons and sit
and talk?"

"Maybe we could do things for you," Mary Jane offered. "Like clean the mice cage and feed the fish and water the plants?"

"My Science Club people are supposed to do that." Mr. Stiller was talking slowly, still thinking.

Mary Jane remembered way back to the first weeks of school when Miss Rousseau had read an announcement about the Science Club. If he had a club like that, why couldn't they join? It couldn't be that Mr. Stiller didn't want her in his club. Or could it? Her eyelids drooped ever so slightly as she made up her mind not to ask.

Mary Jane decided not to ask, but that didn't stop Sally. "Then we'll join the Science Club," she cheerfully announced. "They won't take Mary Jane in cheerleading or me in basketball, but after all, Science — we're good in that. I don't know why we didn't think of it before."

She looked so pleased that Mary Jane was sure Mr. Stiller would say "Yes." Only he didn't. He sat there, absent-mindedly tapping his finger on the window sill. "You can't join the Science Club," he said.

Mary Jane slid off the table she was sitting on, intending to walk toward the door. She hadn't gotten far when Sally asked, "Whyever not?"

"Because it's only for senior high," Mr. Stiller explained.

Mary Jane swallowed hard and bent over to look at the fish, hoping that he hadn't noticed her. Fred kept saying that she was too touchy and she guessed he was right.

"Then why can't we have a Junior Science Club?" Sally persisted.

"I was thinking about that." Mr. Stiller nodded. "I tried to form one a few years ago and there wasn't much interest. But now, with everybody talking about science, we could probably get enough people together. With you two and half a dozen more, that'd be enough for a start."

"Fabulous." Sally beamed her pleasure.

"Tremendous." Mary Jane turned from the fish to smile at Mr. Stiller.

"I'll talk to Mrs. Davis tomorrow and ask her to announce it in the morning bulletin." He nodded again.

"Tomorrow?" Sally looked up at him eagerly. "Couldn't you talk to her about it today? I mean, she was still in her office when we walked by before."

Mr. Stiller laughed. "See here, you two," he warned. "I'll try to catch her today, but don't figure that a science club will solve everything. You'll only have one meeting a week."

"Science Club one day, basketball game another." Sally counted on her fingers. "That leaves just three afternoons to find a place to go."

"Say, what does a science club do?" Mary Jane wondered. "I mean, couldn't we have experiments and stuff that we could work on here other days?"

"Whoah! wait a minute." Mr. Stiller held up his hand, trying to sound stern. "If you work here, I have to stay to keep an eye on you. And I can't stay every single blessed afternoon. There just might be something else I want to do."

"Not every afternoon," Sally reminded him with a grin. "There's the day we watch the basketball game."

Mr. Stiller chuckled. "Good to hear that you'll give me one day off. Now if you'll excuse me, I have an important appointment — "

Before he could finish the sentence, Miss Rousseau appeared in the doorway, Miss Rousseau in a new coat and hat, saying, "I've been waiting for ten minutes," and then, "Hello, you two."

Mr. Stiller looked embarrassed as he explained about the Science-Club-to-be, and Mary Jane and Sally said good-by as quickly as they could. It wasn't hard to figure out that his "important appointment" was Miss Rousseau.

"Do you suppose they're in love?" Sally asked as she stooped down in front of her locker to put on her boots.

"I guess they are," Mary Jane sighed happily. "You should have heard them arguing at the farm. People don't fight like that unless they're at least awfully good friends."

In home room the next morning Miss Rousseau looked straight at Mary Jane when she read the announcement about the Junior Science Club. Mr. Stiller had said that they needed six or eight people to get started, but there were thirteen boys and girls crowding around his desk after school. Most of them were eighth- and ninth-graders, and older than Sally and Mary Jane. One or two of the girls stared curiously at them, but nobody acted unpleasant or said mean things. Everybody was too busy starting a science club.

Before the afternoon was over they had

elected a president and a secretary, agreed on a quarter a month dues, and picked Friday for their regular meeting day. It took two more Fridays to write a constitution and to decide to buy club pins for all the members to wear. After that they were ready to plan things to do.

Trips, somebody suggested. A museum in a neighboring town, a laboratory in High Ridge, a model dairy farm. And in the spring when the weather was nice they could spend Fridays in Calhoun Park collecting frogs' eggs in the pond and hunting for salamanders under the rocks and — Everybody talked at once, proposing places to visit and asking questions, until no one could keep track of what was going on. Everybody talked, that is, except Mary Jane and Sally. Mary Jane drew pictures on the cover of her Science book as if she wasn't even interested in the discussion, while Sally wigwagged frantically, trying to catch Mr. Stiller's attention.

"Hush!" Randall, the president, banged for order. "One at a time," he announced, "so Johnnie May can put it all down in the minutes. We'll go around the room and give everyone a chance to make suggestions."

Mary Jane bent her head, holding tight to

her pencil as she scribbled on her book cover. When he got around to her, what was she going to say? She scarcely listened as Randall called on the boys in the front row and then the girls.

"Mary Jane?"

At last it was her turn. Her heart beat fast as the club members shifted in their seats to look at her. To look at her and then, suddenly, look away again, studying the ceiling and the floor and their fingernails, looking everyplace except at Mary Jane. Sally reddened and even Mr. Stiller had an odd expression on his face.

Somebody had to say something, and after what seemed like hours of silence Mary Jane did. "The places you're talking about, I don't know if I can go. That museum has a special day for colored, and of course the park is out entirely. So you just go ahead and make your plans without me." Her voice cracked a little, but she managed to get it all said, real fast.

The room was quiet after that, so quiet that she could hear the mice racing around on their squeaky exercise wheel. Then there was a hubbub of voices.

"I never thought —"

"Are you sure?"

"What can we do?"

"One at a time." Randall pounded with his fist on Mr. Stiller's desk. "Raise your hand if you want the floor."

A girl sitting on a stool near the window was the first to speak. "If Mary Jane doesn't mind — like she said, let's go ahead and make up our list. I mean, we can't help it about the park and all."

Mary Jane filled in all the *o*'s on her book cover and put little round circles above the *i*'s. Her face felt stiff and cold.

"I think that's mean." It was Johnnie May, the secretary, talking. "After all, what's a club for if it doesn't stick together?"

"But then we won't be able to go anyplace," the girl near the window objected.

"Maybe," one of the boys thought, "if she went with us they'd let her in. Maybe we could ask, write a letter or something."

"Won't do any good," another boy was sure. "But I think — "

Mary Jane hunched over her book, carefully shading the big *W* in "Wilson" while Sally bounced up and down, waving her hand so that Randall would call on her.

"I have something to say," Randall announced. "If anyone had asked me last year, I'd have voted against integration. All my life I heard that Negro kids were — well, you know — " He broke off embarrassed.

Mary Jane looked up at him through her lashes. The freckles on his nose stood out and his cheeks were as red as Sally's.

"But now that we've got it, it doesn't make any difference," he continued. "People like Mary Jane and Fred Jackson, they're just the same as we are. I mean, it's the law and we have to live with it. What I'm trying to say is" — he drew a deep breath — "I don't think the club should go anyplace where Mary Jane can't go."

"Neither do I." Johnnie May nodded agreement.

Mary Jane put her pencil on the table and sat up straight as hands shot up all over the room. It seemed as if everyone wanted to make a motion and second it and take a vote. Pretty soon a motion was made and seconded and passed, eleven for and one against.

Johnnie May wrote it down carefully in the minutes: "Resolved that the Junior Science Club

of Woodrow Wilson High School will make a
list of all the places it wants to visit. Those
places that won't permit Negro students, the
Junior Science Club won't go to."

Science Fair

22

THAT SCIENCE CLUB meeting was far and away
the best thing that had happened to Mary Jane
at Wilson High. It was even better than when
Furry was in school and she had dressed him
up to be mascot at the basketball game. Because this time it wasn't her squirrel they were
accepting, it was her.

Now when the red-haired boy with the water
pistol jostled her in the hall, she gave him a
superior smile and walked on. When Darlene
sniggered or whispered mean things in class,
she said, *"Je m'en moque,"* and watched Darlene hunt for the words in her French vocabulary. In Social Studies, when the teacher said
"your people" and the class turned to look at
her, she craned her neck, too, and kept on doing it until some of the boys and girls laughed.

All thirteen members of the Science Club

went to a laboratory that made penicillin and terramycin and to a factory where milk was pasteurized. But none of them went to the museum which allowed colored visitors only on Tuesdays or to the model farm on the outskirts of High Ridge which didn't allow colored at all.

In between their trips they drew posters about planting trees and eating big breakfasts, to hang on the bulletin boards in the halls. After Christmas vacation they were starting to make a list of speakers to invite to their meetings — doctors like Sally's father and biologists like Grampa — when Mr. Stiller received a letter from the *Evening Chronicle*.

The *Chronicle* wanted to have a science fair in High Ridge. There were state fairs and national ones where the winners got to go to Washington, but these were all for older boys and girls. The *Chronicle* asked if they would be interested in a fair for junior high.

Would they be interested? Johnnie May collected butterflies and moths and cocoons. Randall had a half-finished rocket in his bedroom that his mother said he had to move, and two other boys were building a jet engine for a model plane.

Trips were called off, speakers postponed, and

every single meeting of the club was devoted to planning for the fair. Two ninth-graders decided to build a mechanical brain. One girl started a model of the moon and another was working on a color wheel. Almost every afternoon members of the Science Club wandered into the Science room, looking up things in Mr. Stiller's books and asking for his advice.

Sally and Mary Jane weren't sure what they wanted to do. Mr. Stiller suggested experiments with plants, growing some in water with chemicals and others in peat moss or dirt. Most of the boys in the club thought they ought to build a model of a satellite, and the girls asked if they had considered dinosaurs or a collection of birds' nests.

Sally and Mary Jane turned all the suggestions over in their minds and then turned them down. "Trouble is," Sally explained, "we're mostly interested in live animals."

"Like Furry," Mary Jane sighed.

"How about ants?" Mr. Stiller asked. "You could build an ant house with two pieces of glass and — "

"Too little." Sally shook her head.

"Turtles?"

"Too poky," Mary Jane decided.

Mr. Stiller was growing impatient. "Tropical fish," he proposed in a take-it-or-leave-it voice.

Sally glanced at the aquarium on the window sill. "No-o-o," she answered slowly. "I don't really like fish, not even to eat. But say, how about white mice? I bet my father could get us some from the lab at the hospital."

Mary Jane agreed with a giggle. She couldn't help thinking of how horrified Mamma would be at the very idea. But if she washed her hands carefully before she went home, Mamma couldn't really complain. After all, these were sure to be nice, sanitary mice, coming as they did from a hospital.

Once more the parakeet cage traveled from the Douglases' garage to Wilson High. With Mr. Stiller's help Mary Jane and Sally lined it with wire screening so that the mice couldn't escape through the bars. When it was ready, Sally brought in two mice, plump little animals with twitching pink noses and hairless pink tails.

"Now, what'll we do?" they asked Mr. Stiller. For a science fair, it wasn't enough to keep white mice in a cage. You had to do experiments with them.

"Nutrition," the teacher proposed.

Both girls wrinkled up their noses, not quite sure what "nutrition" meant.

"Can't we do something interesting, teaching them tricks or something?" Sally asked.

"I read about waltzing mice once," Mary Jane said. "Do you suppose — "

Mr. Stiller interrupted with a laugh. "Nobody teaches waltzing mice to waltz. They're born that way. Something's wrong with their ears so that they spin round and round. You couldn't teach your mice to dance, not in a thousand years."

Mary Jane felt so foolish that when Mr. Stiller suggested feeding one mouse seeds and greens and cheese and giving the other only sweets to eat she readily agreed. It took two more afternoons after school to put a divider in the cage so that the boy mouse, who was going to eat regular mouse meals, and the girl mouse, who was going to eat candy, wouldn't get mixed up. At first they named the boy Richard, after Mr. Stiller, and the girl Celeste, after Miss Rousseau, but when Mr. Stiller heard the names he got red in the face and made them change them. Now the mice were called George and Martha, after the Washingtons.

For one whole week George stuffed himself

on birdseed and lettuce and cheese crumbs while Martha nibbled at chocolate bars and lollipops. For one whole week George grew fatter and Martha thinner. George grew frisky and Martha slow, until the girls began to worry about her.

"The experiment's coming along fine," Mr. Stiller reassured them.

"I don't think it's so fine," Sally said. "She gets skinnier and skinnier."

"I feel like a murderer," Mary Jane announced.

Mr. Stiller threw up his hands, pretending to be disgusted. "Some scientists you are," he teased. "If you don't like Martha's looks, you can fatten her up and try something else. But you'd better settle on a project quickly. The fair's just a month away."

"How about a maze?" Randall, sitting at a nearby table, reading about rockets, was interested in their problem. "I saw in a magazine where someone trained mice to go through little doors and runways to find their food. It was real neat."

Mary Jane and Sally approved of the maze, but Mr. Stiller wasn't sure. "Takes a lot of

patience to train a mouse. You'll really have to
stick to it," he warned them.

There were pictures of mazes in one of his
books. Most of them looked too complicated,
but at last they found one with only half a
dozen passageways and dead-end streets that
Mr. Stiller thought could be built into their
cage.

While they were studying the pictures, Randall put down his rocket book and disappeared.
He returned with an armload of boards and a
jigsaw he had borrowed from Shop.

"You'll need these to build the maze," he
said.

Mary Jane lifted her eyebrows. Randall was
funny. He was in the Science room almost every day, reading about rockets. Only sometimes
he stopped reading to stare at her. It wasn't
an unfriendly stare. It was as if he had never
seen anyone like her before and was trying to
figure her out.

For the rest of the week he helped the girls
build the maze. He even cut off the top of the
cage and fastened it back on again with hinges
so that it would be easier for them to reach the
mice. When they thanked him, he shrugged
his shoulders.

"There's four schools going to be in that science fair," he gruffly explained. "You want Wilson's exhibits to be best, don't you?"

At last the maze was completed. Sally held Martha in her hand while Mary Jane started George off on his trip. He was supposed to run along the passageways, turning left and right and left again, until he found a piece of bread.

"Ready, get set, go!" Mary Jane shouted.

Only George didn't go. He sat in the runway, sniffing the bread and looking confused. When he finally started he turned right and left and right again.

"George isn't very smart," Sally announced after he'd made a dozen wrong turns without getting even close to the bread. "Let Martha try."

Martha wasn't very smart either. She twitched her whiskers and made false starts and wrong turns just as George had done. The girls tried singing "Three Blind Mice" to cheer her on until Mr. Stiller, marking papers at his desk, demanded quiet.

There was no longer any question of where they should go after school. Every afternoon, even on days when there were basketball games, Mary Jane and Sally struggled to teach

George and Martha to find their way through the maze. Every afternoon George and Martha sniffed and sat and made wrong turns, looking frightened and confused.

Mr. Stiller counseled patience and Miss Rousseau said, "Rome wasn't built in a day," and Randall, who stopped by to see how they were coming along, didn't say anything at all. Singing "Three Blind Mice" was no longer funny. Mary Jane's neck ached from bending over the cage, and Sally was just plain tired of being patient.

"Only one more try," she announced in disgust. "If one of those beasts doesn't work it today, I quit."

Mary Jane put Martha in the cage. The mouse ran, sat still, sniffed and ran again. She turned left and right and left until she reached the piece of bread! The next afternoon George did the same thing. The mice were slow at first, but after a while they could find the bread without stopping once or making a single mistake.

On the Friday before the fair the Science Club members brought in their exhibits. The tables in the back of the room were crowded with rockets and robots and models of the moon. When the club meeting was over, everyone gathered around to watch the mice run through their maze. Martha was faster, two whole seconds faster when Mary Jane timed her with Mr. Stiller's stop watch, but even George was pretty quick.

Johnnie May asked if she could hold Martha. "You've got a real good chance to win a prize in the fair," she thought.

Mary Jane was surprised. She'd been so busy working with the mice that she hadn't even thought about prizes. She said, "Oh no," politely, the way you were supposed to when people said, "Bet you got an A on that test."

Sally smiled mischievously. She'd been thinking about prizes all along. "Know what'll happen if we win?" she asked the Science Club members. "They'll put our pictures in the paper, the two of us together. After all, the *Chronicle's* running this fair. They'll have to print our pictures. And then what will the Mothers' League say?"

Everyone was quiet for a moment, thinking about how the pictures would look in the *Chronicle*. Thinking that their parents and all the people in High Ridge would see that a little girl with blond hair and a middle-sized girl with skin the color of cinnamon toast could work together and be friends.

Randall broke the silence with a laugh. "Certainly be different from that picture of Darlene and you, the first day of school," he told Mary Jane. "But even if you don't win, we ought to put up a big sign over your exhibit. For all the visitors at the fair to see."

"What'll the sign say?" Johnnie May asked.

"What'll it say?" Randall grinned. "IF WHITE MICE CAN LEARN, SO CAN YOU."

He was joking, of course, but Mary Jane was pleased. She didn't really care if the mice won a prize in the science fair. When Randall, who was a boy in ninth grade and president of the Science Club, could make a joke like that, she felt warm from the fluff on her forehead all the way down to the tips of her toes. Because in spite of Darlene and Sharon and Miss Collins and the redheaded boy with the water pistol, she guessed she was succeeding as foreign ambassador at Wilson High after all.